BURLESQUE ON BOURBON

Burlesque River – Book Two

Kitty Bardot

PRAISE FOR BURLESQUE RIVER

Burlesque River

"This was one of the most beautiful love stories. Mike and Amanda have been friends and together since she was 11 years old. After high school they were set to marry, but Amanda's rough childhood compared to Mike's normal family life weighed to heavily on her and she never felt good enough for Mike. For 12 years the both floated along, never finding love or anything close to what they had. When Amanda's Burlesque troupe performs at Mike's bar completely by chance, the two are reunited and feelings come flooding back. Emotional struggles are hard enough, but Amanda has a secret that can tear them apart. Four steamy days together bring these two on quite the roller coaster and we get to go along for the ride. Beautiful, emotional, perfect." ~MidnightMaiden

"I haven't read many romance novels, but the few I have read lack the depth of emotion on display in Kitty Bardot's Burlesque River. *Bardot tells the story of young lovers, Amanda and Mike, separated by life's unique cruelty, thrown back together 12 years later. Mistakes are made, arguments are had, and the lovers are forced to deal with the ramifications of their actions, some of which have left terrible scars. Also...in true romance novel style there is a lot of sex and a lot of different kinds of sex, always a good thing in a book like this. Most significantly though, there is a literary thrust (no pun intended) to it that elevates* Burlesque River *above similar novels. I, for one, can't wait for the sequel."* ~Kimberly

"Even though it was an easy read, there was a great depth to the characters and story line. Not to mention this book is hot, hot, hot. I really enjoyed it, and can't wait for book number 2." ~MrsBates2U

"Romance is not my usual thing but I picked this up and ended up devouring it in two days. The love story is heartfelt, the sex is passionate, and the characters are all lovable and real. Definite recommend and I'm looking forward to the next book in the series!" ~Joshua Kahn

www.BOROUGHSPUBLISHINGGROUP.com

BURLESQUE ON BOURBON
Copyright © 2020 Kitty Bardot

ISBN: 978-1-953810-07-6

To my husband again, and always.
Thank you for being my real-life hero.
To Lindsay, my other-other half.
And to my burlesque sisters and brothers who inspire me daily.
Life would be terribly dull without you all.

ACKNOWLEDGMENTS

Special thanks to my editor for all the phone calls, edits, and encouragement. This book wouldn't be what it is without you.

BURLESQUE ON BOURBON

Chapter 1

"This isn't quite how I remember it," Bridgette says to Bunny as they ride along Canal Street. Their Uber driver is speeding and weaving through a riot of motorized vehicles and people. Something's aching in Bridgette's chest as she looks out at New Orleans, one of her favorite cities. Though she's sure it hasn't changed much since her childhood trips, it feels off. Broken storefronts and empty buildings have made way for designer and discount stores. Mixed in with those are chain restaurants and gas stations.

"What do you mean?" Bunny asks. "This is exactly how I imagined it."

"It's so new and modern. I remember it differently. It was like travelling back in time. All the old houses and restaurants, the broken sidewalks… This feels wrong. Like a bad dream in some places. Or like it's been washed and pressed in others."

"I don't know what you're seeing. This place is wrinkled as fuck." Bunny gestures around as their car halts suddenly and a streetcar zips by, arms hanging out the open windows. She laughs, eyes wide, shaking her head with a grin. "I love it."

Bridgette smiles at her surrogate big sister and leans back into her seat. "I wish you could see it the way I remember it. When my grandparents would bring me here as a kid. It was magical. We'd drive down from Illinois always in the early spring. It was like driving into summer on another planet. I'd watch the cold gray countryside slip away into the wet green of the south. Tennessee smelled like sawdust, and I'd try to count all the logs that were stacked up along the road. Then, as we hit the highway, high up over the water, giant naked trees would reach out of the swamp—" Bridgette shuts up as their car turns abruptly and they slide into each other in the backseat. Her heart is racing.

"Jesus. You must need some kind of special license to drive in this town," Bunny exclaims, scooting back to her side of the car, holding the grip above her head. "Or none at all," she whispers, teeth bared in a look of sheer terror as the streets narrow around them. Cars are parked on either side, and with work crews and pedestrians, it seems like a one-lane street. Though the oncoming traffic doesn't notice. Their car slows and stops in front of a gleaming white building over ten stories tall.

"Is this it?" Bridgette ask, her eyes wide with awe.

"Hotel Mon-te-leone?" Bunny responds with poor pronunciation, ducking down to read the sign above the door through the car window. "Yep."

"Damn Mike. He sure knows how to treat you."

"Yeah, he does," Bunny agrees. "When I told him you were performing down here, he jumped at the opportunity to book everything. He'll be down tomorrow to join us."

"This is awesome. I was going to stay with Lilian otherwise. She said she had plenty of room." Bridgette's grateful for the hotel. Even a modest one would be better than sleeping at a stranger's place. No amount of trust could make the first night in another person's home an easy one. She liked routine. She valued her own space. It's exactly why she paid more than anyone else for a private room at the town house in Chicago. She loved her burlesque family, but needed a space of her own. A space to be alone. It wasn't any different here or anywhere she travelled. When she'd accepted the invite to perform in New Orleans, she had dreaded the idea of staying with Lilian.

"As fun as I'm sure that would be, I think we might prefer this." Bunny smiles and hops out of the car, thanking their driver. He pops the trunk. Before Bridgette is done thanking and tipping him, a bellhop appears with a cart to collect their bags. They both hurry to help him load their things. "Thank you so much," they say in unison and laugh. The hot, wet southern air is pulling at their clothes. The noise of traffic bustles all around, and the scent of the Mississippi wafts around them, heavy, musty, and full of secrets.

"Welcome to New Orleans, ladies," he says with a broad smile and shining face. "And welcome to the Hotel Monteleone." He pushes the heavily loaded cart through the double doors. The lobby is cool and peaceful, a relief to Bridgette's overwhelmed senses. As much as she longs to see the world, flying and airports drain her.

Antique furniture in sumptuous earth tones dots the lobby around low coffee tables under golden lights. An elderly couple sit, looking over a city map, talking in low voices. Bridgette's reminded of her grandparents. A smile warms her face.

"This is how I remember it." She speaks softly, breathing in the smell of antiquity. Her racing heart slows.

***

"Oh my God, Bunny, this is amazing," Bridgette squeals, standing in the sitting room of their suite. The air conditioning is blowing cool air over the sumptuous furnishings and appointments. Heavy gold damask drapes are tied back with braided cords at the end of which hang thick gold and black tassels. The bright afternoon light makes the suite glow.

"It is. I wish Mike was here though," Bunny whines from the golden velour couch. She uncorks a bottle of champagne and pours them each a glass. Then she digs through her suitcase lying open on the polished-to-a-high-shine coffee table.

"You'll be fine," Bridgette says in a patronizing tone. "It's only for one night." She rolls her eyes and sits next to her friend, tossing a plush burgundy pillow onto the wingback chair to her left. "Besides, it wasn't all that long ago that you tried to leave him," she teases, sipping her champagne.

"Don't remind me," Bunny says with a sigh. "Long past. That was over two years ago." She relaxes into her pillow, looking out the window to the French Quarter below.

Bridgette looks out too. Reminiscing about her childhood trips with her grandparents, she watches the champagne bubbles rolling up the crystal flute. Fine crystal and premium champagne are a far cry from the plastic cups wrapped in cellophane in the modest hotels they would stay in on the outskirts of the city. She remembers driving in for the day's sightseeing adventures. How she had wondered what the fancy hotels in the Quarter were like on the inside. And here she is sitting in a luxurious suite, courtesy of Bunny's lover. "Besides, the man's gotta work to keep spoiling you like this," she says, a small pang of jealousy washed down with a large swallow of dry, fizzy goodness.

"That's the thing, Bridgette, he doesn't. He's got more money than either one of us can imagine." She shakes her head and lowers her voice to sound like him. "Sound investments." She giggles. "He says that all the time. I don't fucking know how he makes his money, but he does spoil me."

"You're telling me. Look around. It's almost as big as our main floor back home." Bridgette gestures to their decadent surroundings in one wide sweep of the arm. "It's pretty great of him to put us up for the weekend though. This place is amazing."

"It is, but it *would* be better if he were here with us."

"Maybe for you. But then I'd be alone in my room, while you two wrecked this suite. This way we get a girls' night in New Orleans, *before* you wreck the suite."

"You're right," Bunny says, looking through the French doors to the antique four-poster bed with a dreamy smile.

"Goddammit, Bunny," Bridgette shouts. "Get it together, ho. I can read your mind and you're sick."

"Sick with love." Bunny laughs with a slight blush to her cheeks and starts looking through her suitcase again.

Bridgette watches her friend and wonders what it would be like to be so madly in love. Sure, she'd been heartbroken when Bunny left their shared home in Chicago. The whole troupe had, really. But seeing how happy she is with Mike, how he completes her in a way that no one thought possible, is something beautiful. Something Bridgette longs to find herself someday.

"So, what do we know about this Lilian chick anyway?" Bunny asks, standing to change.

"Well, she's got a studio space in the Quarter, and a small group of dancers that perform together in the area. It's not a troupe, officially. But from what I've gathered, they may as well be."

"Cool. When are we meeting up with her?"

"I told her we'd be there around six or so."

"Sweet, that gives us time to explore."

After they finish their champagne, freshen up and change, they go downstairs and hit the street, where the sights and sounds of the city surround them. The heat is overwhelming, but it doesn't stop people who are walking in every direction. Bridgette's mind floats on a champagne cloud. She smooths her fine hair back from her already sweating forehead.

"This heat though. Why did I think it would be the same as back home?" Bunny asks, pulling her hair into a messy bun.

"It pretty much is. Only wetter, stickier…and hotter."

"Hey there, young ladies," someone calls from behind them. They turn to look. The guy staggers toward them, a small bottle of whiskey in his hand. His dirty clothes hang from his slight frame. "I bet, I bet I can tell you where you got them shoes," he slurs. "I bet you five dollars I know where you got those shoes." He gestures to their feet.

"I'm sorry, what?" Bridgette snaps, her heart rate rising, her pulse thumping in her ears. She's already on guard from the throngs of people milling about. The heat and champagne aren't helping her maintain her cool.

"Those shoes. Both pairs. Yours and hers," he shouts with an air that only a drunk can muster. "Five dollars I can tell you where you got them."

She looks him over from faded hat to ragged shoes. She can see the dirt caked under his nails on the hand gripping the cheap bottle of whiskey. It's running low. Her irritation becomes pity. She reaches into her purse for the money. Before she has her wallet in hand, the doorman appears between them, guiding the vagrant away.

"I'm sorry, ma'am," he calls over his shoulder as he urges the man along.

"It's okay," she says, embarrassed for the man being led away like a child.

"C'mon, Bridgette," Bunny says from her side. "Let's head this way."

"Okay," she responds with a soft voice, wondering what would lead a man to a life like that. Drunk and filthy, harassing strangers for money.

"Hey," Bunny says. "It's sad, but there's nothing you could do for him."

"I know. He was so dirty, and he looked like he's given up on life."

"He probably has," Bunny says as they walk along.

"You're right. Sad," Bridgette responds, pulling her purse across her chest, securing it in front of her body. "I guess the only difference between here and home is that it's legal to carry whiskey bottles on the street."

"Plus, it's warm most of the year."

"Yeah," Bridgette agrees, suddenly uncomfortable with the luxury of her life. She's never been desperate, never given up. Not like that. Things haven't always been easy, but here she is staying in a beautiful hotel with her best friend, plenty of money for the weekend, getting paid to dance in a costume that's worth more in rhinestones than that guy surely sees in a month.

"Hey." Bunny bumps her gently with her shoulder as they stroll down Royal Street toward Jackson Square. "Let's go in here." She gestures to the yellow wooden sign hanging above a black door. "The Voodoo Bone Lady Shop and Psychic Readings," she says with a spooky cadence, wiggling her fingers in the air.

"Yes," Bridgette agrees.

A bell rings as they push through the door. Inside there are dark corners and dusty floors. The heavy smell of burning incense permeates the air. A sign propped against the wall assures that The Voodoo Bone Lady has your best interests at heart. The walls are covered with masks and portraits. On the counters are candles, trinkets, vials of creams and potions, and voodoo dolls wrapped with twine, made of curious materials.

Shelves hold books old and new, a variety of tarot decks, and blank leather-bound journals. Skulls and other bones fill the open spaces. An altar stands on one wall, loaded down with many of the items that are for sale in the shop. There's also an array of personal things. Pictures of loved ones, notes folded on torn pieces of paper, and unscratched lottery tickets, bills and coins from all around the world, cigarettes, and what looks like a hand-rolled joint.

The longer Bridgette looks the more she sees. A small sign posted for all to see warns customers not to touch the altar with a mention of Papa Legba. Upon closer inspection, she sees fingernail clippings and locks of hair, a small glass bottle of something long since dried and brown. A chill runs up her back, tingling her scalp.

The bell on the door rings as folks leave and enter. She's lost in the array of wishes spread out before her and drawn to leave an offering. With nothing in her possession she's willing to part with, she takes a slip of torn parchment from the stack provided and places her lips to it. Pressing the sheer pink gloss to the paper, she asks for nothing, only stands in reverence of the power of belief. So many people left something of themselves here. Now she had as well. *Here's to you, Papa,* she thinks in a whisper, as she places the barely visible kiss among so many promises and wishes.

"You gotta be careful when you're dealing with Papa Legba, *cher.*" A soft, deep, masculine Southern voice speaks from behind her. Bridgette jumps and turns to see its source. He's standing tall and lean, impeccably dressed. Not a single black hair out of place. His shining eyes are almost as dark as he smiles down at her with a playful air of mystery. She stammers, her cheeks warming with embarrassment for being caught in such a childish act. All words get lost before they hit her tongue.

The bell on the door rings as it's opened again. The afternoon sun shines in, casting him in a ray of golden light. The dust in the air shimmers around him like glitter. He raises one finger to his smirking lips. "Shhh. Keep your secrets." She can't tell if he's making fun of her. She can, however, feel an undeniable attraction to him. She wants to touch his perfect hair or stroke the soft fabric of his shirt. He's like something from a dream, materialized in reality for one enchanted moment. As they stand in silent courtship, Bridgette struggles to find words.

"Henri," the man behind the counter shouts from across the small shop. His low, booming voice shatters the dreamy reverie that hung between her and the mysterious Henri, who nods and turns his attention to the man who called him.

"Oooh. How'd I miss this?" Bunny asks, sliding up to the altar beside her. "This is some spooky shit," she whispers, pointing to some of the less savory items laid out as offerings.

"You're telling me," Bridgette says, admiring the straight, confident lines of Henri's shoulders as he leans against the counter in conversation with the man who called him. Henri looks over to her and offers another gleaming smile.

Following Bridgette's gaze and admiring his handsome frame, Bunny asks under her breath, "And how'd I miss that?"

"Not sure," Bridgette says and shivers with the feeling of something strange. "Come on though. We should get moving." She heads for the door. With the jingle of the bells, they are back on the street under the bright sun. The oppressive heat and throngs of people are no distraction as she tries to shake the feelings from the encounter.

She's not sure she wants to.

***

Henri rambles along Royal Street. He dodges and weaves through tourists as they look in every direction except the one they're going. They pour in and out of shops selling the same tacky t-shirts, shot glasses, and Mardi Gras beads as the shops before them. Though he has a distaste for all the commercialism, he loves the people. Their wide-eyed appreciation of everything he loves about his city is endearing. No matter how foolish, drunk, and bloated they seem in their ongoing pursuit of the town's next thrill, he embraces their presence. *After all, without them, what would the city be?*

The demo he carries in his hand is an answer to his question. Music. A language that transcends all barriers. A good musician could make you feel something in any language. Jo was one of those musicians. Henri had, after years of trying, finally gotten him into the studio to record. Those recordings were pure magic. Jo had a sound so original it had a purity that couldn't be ignored. Somehow dark and uplifting at once, a juxtaposition that could only be born in the streets of New Orleans. As Henri considers every nuance of the man's talent, he enters the shop where Jo works his day job.

Inside the Bone Woman's shop, trinkets and souvenirs of a more frightening nature greet him. Jo stands behind the counter talking with a customer. Across the room, standing at the altar, is a sight to behold. Light jean cutoffs sitting comfortably on tan hips, exposing the bottom of a brightly colored tattoo on her upper thigh. A white top, not much more than fringe, shows off tattooed shoulders and delicate forearms. Her silken, sun-streaked hair lies across her bare back. As she turns to reach for something, he catches her profile. Her face is as soft and sweet as the rest of her. With a perfect nose, lips full and glossy, cheeks that beg to be caressed.

In a moment of innocence and ecstasy, she places a small sheet of paper to her lips. With her eyes closed, she holds it there for the rise and fall of one poetic breath. It would be brazen to approach her there at that moment, but Henri can't help himself. He's drawn to her.

He crosses the room. "You gotta be careful when you're dealing with Papa Legba, *cher*," he all but whispers near her. She jumps with a start and turns his way, blushing and stammering. She's a goddamn angel. Standing in the middle of a voodoo shop, making the most sensual offering she possibly could. Henri is taken off guard by her absolute beauty, her sparkling brown eyes.

He smiles as he searches for his voice and forces himself to play it cool. Raising a finger to his lips, he says, "Shhh. Keep your secrets." For the moment, they are the only two in the room. The ringing bells, the bustle of bodies around them, it all falls away. Then it's broken, in an instant, by the booming voice of Jo Crane. He nods to her and turns away, thankful for an excuse to do so. Once he collects himself, he can make a proper introduction.

"Henri. How's it going, man?" Jo asks as he approaches the counter. "Done with this already?" Jo chuckles as Henri slides the demo CD across the counter. Jo stands a few inches shorter than him and is as dark as a man can be. Though they've known each other for years, Henri still can't guess his age.

"You're going to be so pleased when you listen. You'll hear what I've been talkin' about this whole time," Henri says, turning back to admire his mystery woman. She's joined by a friend who's taller and older. Maybe a sister.

"Couple of nice ones there, eh?"

"You're telling me. There are beautiful women everywhere in this town. But that one there. She's a goddamn angel. I've gotta go properly introduce myself."

"Too late, friend." Jo nods toward the door as it jingles.

"Listen to this," Henri says quickly, tapping the demo case. "I'll come to see you at the club later tonight. But for now, I've got to chase that woman." He rushes from the darkened shop into the bright daylight. Looking left and right through the never-ending onslaught of people, he doesn't see her. She's gone. He wanders in one direction, then the other, stretching his neck, looking through every break in the crowd.

She's gone. *How did she disappear so quickly? Where could she be? Why didn't you introduce yourself? If I had just gotten a name… Anything.*

He enters the shop next door. She's not there. The one next to that. Nothing. Two more shops in either direction and he's back where he started. Standing in the middle of the thoroughfare, looking in every direction like a madman.

"No luck?" Jo steps up from behind him.

Henri shakes his head. Together they walk toward Jackson Square. "Touring today?"

"Yep. I'm heading to meet the group now. Wanna join?"

"No, I think I'll head home for a bit," Henri says.

"You ain't going home." Jo laughs.

"What are you saying? You think I'm going to wander around the Quarter looking for her all night?"

"Well?" Jo asks with both eyebrows raised, sliding his hands in his pockets.

"I might take the long way home. Give Bourbon Street a once-over."

"Yeah, that's what I thought." Jo chuckles. "Millions of women walk down these streets every year. I've never seen you chase one."

"I've never seen one worth chasing." Henri grins at the thought of finding her again. He wonders about her name, her life. Where is she from? What brought her here? And right now, most importantly, where did she go?

Chapter 2

"I don't know, Bunny. That guy, there was something about him." They walk through the busy streets of the French Quarter.

"You're telling me," Bunny says, nudging Bridgette in the ribs. "You think we'll see him again?"

"Probably not. This is a crazy place. People are coming and going every day of the week. He could be gone tomorrow or even this afternoon. There's no way of finding him. I think his name was Henri. He had the most amazing accent."

"Well, maybe we will see him around."

"Maybe." They walk in silence. Bridgette's mind is back in the shop. "I mean, the way he looked at me like he knew my secrets. Like he knew me inside and out. I had left a kiss for Papa Legba on the altar and Henri appeared like magic. I know it's silly. But I think I made a deal with the devil."

Bunny's laughter rises over the noisy street. "Sorry, Bridgette. He's a handsome devil, for sure. But *the* devil? C'mon."

"Not *him*. The altar, the kiss, Papa Legba."

"I'm following. Did you ask for a sexy Southern affair?"

"I didn't ask for anything. I sort of did what I felt like I should do. It was weird, like I was taken by the moment. I don't know. Then Henri appeared from out of nowhere."

"Like magic?" Bunny says with a smirk.

"Don't make fun of me," Bridgette snaps, punching her arm.

"I'm sorry." Bunny's stifling another laugh.

"Shut up, Bunny."

"Okay, for real though. Maybe it's this Louisiana heat."

"Maybe. Or maybe you're a jerk."

"That may be true. But I'm the only jerk you got."

"Not for long," Bridgett says, stopping, double-checking the address on her phone. "We're here."

"You sure?" Bunny looks at the doorway with some apprehension.

"The address matches the one in her email." They're standing before a faded red door, around the corner from the main road. Its streaky paint covers the glass window at the top as well. On the cracked and broken steps, someone spray-painted the address in sloppy white numbers. Bridgette imagines the stairway on the other side going down to the depths of the city and beyond. "Lemme shoot her a message real quick. Let her know we're here."

"That's a good idea. Have them meet us in the daylight. What do you *really* know about this Lilian lady anyway?"

"We met on a burlesque group on Facebook, started chatting and sharing performance videos a year or so ago. I was telling her how much I love New Orleans and she told me to come down and perform with her. I know she's from Missouri, divorced, and living her best life down here."

"So, she's a real person, for sure?"

"Yes, she's a real person," Bridgette says with an angry eye roll. They wait for a response from Lilian.

"I'm sorry," Bunny says. "It's kinda spooky here, in the alley. I know you did your research. But I mean…"

"It's okay. This *is* a little strange. We'll wait to hear back from her."

The door swings inward, and a woman looking more like a mad scientist than a dancer stands in the doorway wearing an oversize kimono in pink, gold, and blue. It's open wide to reveal men's boxer shorts and an undershirt. Heavy-rimmed glasses sit on her nose, hiding most of her face. Her bleached-blonde with faded-blue hair is pulled up in a knot of the top of her head, bobbing around over the closely shaved sides. "Baby La Loop. Ahhh. Get in here. I finally get to hug you." Her voice has a charming, masculine quality to it.

"Oh, thank god. Yes." Bridgette hurries to embrace her new friend. "I was worried for a second there. I didn't know if this was the place."

"Yeah, it's kinda creepy. But I like it that way. Keeps the weirdos out. Hah."

"Lilian, this is Amanda, everyone calls her Bunny."

"Hey, hey. Get in here too." Lilian pulls Bunny into a big friendly hug as well. "Let's get upstairs. It's hot as fuck out here."

She looks out at the sky as though it's offended her. The heat follows them as they ascend the poorly lit, narrow stairway. Lilian speaks over her shoulder as she shuffles up in bare feet. "Sorry about all the stairs. It's a hell of a workout." Bridgette wonders whether they're escaping the heat at all. It's getting hotter with each step. "Almost there," Lillian calls back. At the top of the stairs are two doors and one naked bulb mounted on the wall. "All right, guys, welcome to Studio One." She pushes the door to the left wide open. The cold air hits them instantly as they reach the landing. The scent of pot and perfumed candles greets them. The light is low coming from a dozen standing lamps, some antique with blown glass shades and intricate brass work, others simple and modern. They surround couches and chairs, all of a similar mix. The floors are spread with rugs of every color and shape.

"Oooh... New friends," someone calls from one of the couches. She's reclined seductively, joint in hand. Another woman sits sideways in the chair beside the couch, flipping through a magazine. Her tiny feet hang over the arm of the vintage wingback. "Come here and sit with us." The one lounging welcomes them, sitting up and smoothing the couch beside her. "You must be Baby," she says, offering her joint. Bridgette takes it, welcoming the familiar taste. She fills her lungs and holds it in.

"Thank you," she says before exhaling. "I needed this." Another hit and she passes it back. "I am Baby."

"I'm Charley. This is Trixie Van Stamp," Charley says, handing the joint to Trixie in the chair.

"Hey." She smiles a genuine smile but stays invested in her magazine.

"This is Amanda, everyone calls her Bunny," Bridgette says, relaxing into the couch, reveling in the high.

"Hellllloo, Bunny," Charley coos. "You want this?" She offers the joint. Her every movement dripping with sensuality, every word a song. Amanda takes it and settles in beside Bridgette. Lilian sits cross-legged on the empty couch next to them.

"I'm glad we're finally meeting."

"Me too," Bridgette says. They sit in a comfortable silence, passing one joint after another. The smoke rises to the ceiling. It swirls some sixteen feet above them. Conversations start and stop with ease. The room is huge beyond the light from the lamps. Behind

Lilian are racks of costumes. Past that, Bridgette sees a bed and vanity with more lamps, and beyond that more racks of clothes. Then, it's darkness and open space. The windows are painted at the top. Canvas tarps cover the bottoms, blocking out the sun and the heat.

"So, where ya guys staying?" Lilian asks.

"Hotel Monteleone," Bridgette answers, doing her best at pronunciation.

"Damn, got it like that, huh?"

"Bunny's a bit spoiled over here." She motions to her friend dozing beside her. "Got herself a sugar daddy."

"He's not a sugar daddy," she mumbles in defense and sits up, rubbing her eyes.

"He's got you up at the Monteleone. So, I mean... I worked there once. The bar is pretty sweet."

"Sugar daddy implies that he's old and keeps me with money." Bunny yawns. "I'd be with him if he lived in a shack by the river." She smacks her lips and leans back into the couch. "He keeps me with that dick." She laughs, flat and short. "I'm hungry."

"Speaking of dick," Bridgette jabs.

"I could definitely go for a taste right about now. But I need food. Besides, don't act like you weren't salivating earlier today."

"Fuck you."

"You started it."

"Hey." Charley sits up beside them. "I'll fuck you both." She smiles and leans in close.

"Charlotte is our resident cat in heat," Lilian states. "She will fuck you both. Hah." Bridgette looks down at Charley's hand on her knee. Everything about her is dainty and refined, from her upturned nose to her smiling eyes. She stands and crosses the room, her sheer dress revealing her delicate curves. Mischief and grace in her every step. Bridgette entertains the idea as she watches her walk. What would it be like to touch what's under that dress? To feel Charley's smooth feminine skin against her own? Bridgette's cheeks warm with a subtle blush, and she's thankful for the low lights.

"If you guys are hungry, I know a place nearby. Not too touristy and good food, cheap," Trixie says from her chair. Some of the only words she's spoken since they arrived. "Po'boys and burgers and stuff." She stands up and is surprisingly short. Her tank top and gym shorts are stretched tight over ample curves. Her shining black hair is thick and wavy, reaching her shoulders. It reminds Bridgette of her mystery man, with the same color and shine. She sighs and wonders at the chances of seeing him again.

"Yes, Trixie. Yes. You are my favorite person in the world right now. I will follow you wherever you go," Bunny says, the stoned cadence of her voice giving Bridgette a laugh.

"Sweet," she responds. "Lil, can I borrow a dress? I don't want to go out in this and don't want to go all the way home to change."

"Sure, have at it." Lilian stands and shuffles to the wall. "Brace yourselves, it's about to get real bright in here." She flips a couple of switches and the overhead lights shine bright and unnatural over everything. The dreamy, smoky magic of the afternoon disappears with a flash. The loft is much larger than Bridgette had assessed. "You guys want a tour?"

"Yeah." They both stand, and Lilian leads the way. They pass the first set of racks into the area with the bed. It's cozier than it looked from the couch, made up with fluffy pillows and soft blankets. The vanity, dresser, and what looks like an altar similar to the one at the voodoo shop make up one wall; the many racks of clothes make up the other two. There is no fourth wall. It's open to the other side. "Here's my room," Lilian says as they pass by. On the other side of all the clothes and costumes is a huge open space, making a large L. One end is loaded with props and backdrops, the other (nearest the bed) is open and lined with mirrors. More props and masks hang on the other wall. "This is where we practice. If you wanna use the space before the show tomorrow, I'll be here most of the day." Bridgette and Bunny look at one another, eyes wide with appreciation.

"This is amazing," Bridgette says. Their tiny town house in Chicago, packed with people and stuff, is one third the size of this place. Maybe a quarter. Since Bunny moved, they scored a little more space. But nothing like this.

"It really is," Bunny agrees.

"It sure beats the life I was living in Hannibal," Lilian answers with a sneer. She's looking at her reflection in the wall of mirrors. "Y'all wouldn't recognize Anna Carl if she was standing right next to me." She shakes her head with a sigh of melancholy. "It's amazing what a change of address will do for a person." She smiles and heads to her room to pull on a baggy pair of jeans over her men's underwear.

Bridgette is so curious about the women they've met. Having known Lilian from social media, she knew only the parts of her story she shared with the world. But now that they had met in person, Bridgette wants to know all of it. The real parts Lilian doesn't share with acquaintances on the internet. Bridgette wonders about Charley and Trixie too. Charley, so sexy and confident. Trixie, somehow friendly and aloof at the same time. It's true what she's always believed. Burlesque brought together the best kind of people.

Chapter 3

"This place is full of asshats," Bridgette shouts over the throngs of people. The air is pink and shimmering with neon lights. Bass pumps out of open doorways. The modern club music is out of place on the worn streets. Bodies press in from every angle. It's overwhelming and nothing like the jazz-filled streets of her imagination. She pushes through to a clearing.

"Yeah it is," Lilian answers, nodding her head with vigor. "But, hey, it's Bourbon," she says, spreading her arms wide and spinning around. Behind them, Bunny walks arm in arm with Charley. There's a natural comfort to the way their steps are synced. Charley is speaking low in Bunny's ear. Trixie's walking behind them, sipping from a comically large hurricane glass. "You said you wanted the full experience. Sorry to say, this is it. A whole lot of drunk frat boys shouting from balconies. Actually, a whole lot of drunk folks in general."

"I'm sorry, it's so obnoxious. I mean, thanks for bringing me out." She breathes in the smell of stale urine and chokes back a retch. "But I'm done with this," Bridgette says, pulling her hair off her sweat-moistened neck again. Her anxiety is playing its familiar song in her mind. She's tense and angry, ready to shout, or run, or cry. She remembers her childhood trips, walking down the same street in the daytime, overwhelmed by all the people, but safe because her tiny hand was held firmly in the giant, warm, calloused hand of her grandpa. She releases her clenched fists and relaxes the muscles in her neck and shoulders.

"Hey, no apologies. This shit sucks. Let's go in here." Lilian motions to a quiet-looking place with only a handful of people. The lights are low. It looks cool and inviting.

"Yes. Please. That looks wonderful." Her sigh is heavy with relief as they stand waiting for the others to catch up.

"Ooh, are we going in here? I love this place," Charley coos, leading Bunny by the hand. Trixie follows.

"C'mon. They always have good music in here," Lilian says, tilting her head toward the doorway. Bridgette follows as Lilian leads them to a round booth in the back corner. It's dark, almost private, and perfect. Bridgette can feel herself relaxing as her eyes adjust. "It's still early for anyone to be playing. But we can chill here and have a couple drinks while we wait."

"Perfect. I need a break from out there."

"This is a good place for that. What's everyone having? I'll get the first round." Drinks are ordered and Bridgette settles in beside Trixie. Bunny's next to her with Charley on the outside. Lilian returns with some of their order and heads back to the bar for the rest. "This is a good night to be here. Jo Crane is playing. He's got some good stuff. A real sexy Southern sound. The kinda shit you expect to hear in New Orleans. Not the club garbage they play everywhere else."

"I'm looking forward to it. Thank you." Bridgette takes her drink from Lilian, settles in, and sips slowly. The vodka cranberry is an easy cocktail to drink. Stronger than it tastes and smooth going down.

Bridgette looks around the bar. Low lights create an air of mystery. The booth they're in is faded and worn. The walls are dark and glistening, like the walls of a cave. The stage is to the right of the large bar in the center of the place, and is brightly lit and empty. They're tucked away in the corner, unseen and unheard.

"I'm looking forward to tomorrow night," Lilian says, seating herself on a chair across from them all. "It should be a good show. We'll be performing between two bands. As our guest, you'll be closing."

"Awesome. I should probably take it easy tonight then."

"Ah. Don't take it easy. It's not a fucking school night. Besides, the show doesn't start until after nine anyway. This city sleeps the days away, not the nights."

"She's a terrible influence," Charley calls from across the table.

"The same could be said of you," Lilian says, looking at her arm draped over Bunny's shoulder.

"We're fine over here. Right, Bunny?" Charley asks with a laugh, resting her other hand above Bunny's knee.

"Yeah, don't worry about her," Bridgette says. "She's addicted to that sugar daddy or dick daddy or whatever she wants to call him,"

"It's true, Charley. He is my A-dick-tion." Bunny laughs.

"Jesus, Bunny. I can't take you anywhere." Bridgette rolls her eyes.

"You called him my dick daddy. Where was I supposed to take it?"

"Well, I for one can't wait to meet this dick daddy. He sounds lovely," Charley coos.

"Oh, he is. I bet he likes the name dick daddy too. Don't you think, Bridgette?"

"I wouldn't begin to think about the names you call each other behind closed doors," Bridgette teases.

"Probably best." Bunny chuckles. "Next round's on me."

"I'll help," Charley sings and stands up. Bunny follows her to the bar. Bridgette watches as they stroll away. Someone is taking a seat on stage. The guitar and the man speaking sound like New Orleans.

***

The lights are up on Bourbon, and people are everywhere. Henri enters the quietest club on the busy street. He takes a seat at the bar, ordering a rum and coke. Jo walks over to him in his lightweight cream-colored suit. "No luck with the lady?" he asks, settling on the barstool beside him. Henri can't get her out of his mind, and it's clear to his old friend.

"Nope," Henri answers, finishing his drink in one swallow and motioning for the bartender to get them a round. "She evaporated. I mean, how could someone disappear so quickly? I went into every shop on Royal, every bar, every restaurant. I looked like a lunatic." His words were falling out with a quickness he hates. They remind him of his youth, the youngest sibling, always trying to get the words out before someone cut him off. The frustration of his evening spent searching for his mystery woman is wearing on him. Usually, he gets what he wants. Money does that for a person. It has a dirty magic about it that throws open every door. Most doors, that is.

"Did you listen to the demo?" Henri asks, trying to push her out of his mind.

"Hmm?" Jo hums, sipping his drink. "Ah, not yet." He holds up a finger and sips it again. "I will though. I promise. It's been a busy day, you know. What with the angels in the shop and whatnot."

"Don't patronize me. I'm not in the mood." Henri takes another long drink and glances out the door. "She was an angel, though, wasn't she?"

Jo's eyes narrow as he takes another sip. "I have a feeling you're going to see her again." He stands up and carries his drink to the stage. Settling onto a stool behind the microphone, he picks up his guitar. That familiar bluesy, country twang peels from the strings as his fingers dance over them. "This one's for you, Henri," Jo says into the microphone with a smirk. "Don't be sad."

Henri shakes his head and takes another large swig. As he leans back against the bar, he lets the music do what it does best. Though, when he closes his eyes, there she is in his memory, swaying those luscious hips and giggling.

"Hey, handsome." A smooth soft voice breaks through his reverie. Henri opens his eyes to two lovely faces. Beautiful women with laughter in their words. The blonde smiles like she has a secret. He's sure he knows her, but rum has a way of slowing you down. "Can I buy you a drink, Henri? Is it?"

"I'm sorry, do I know you?"

"Nope." She giggles.

"How do you know my name?"

"You look like a Henri." Another giggle. Henri searches her face for something, anything to jar his memory. She leans in close and whispers. "Do you believe in voodoo?" He sits up quickly. Her hint was enough. She was there, in the shop that afternoon, with his mystery woman who must be there, somewhere. All his searching, and then there was Jo, fucking Jo. He must've seen her come in. He must've known she was there the whole time. Henri takes a breath to calm himself, putting on his best Southern charm.

"Seems unfair you know my name and I don't know yours."

"So, it is Henri."

"It is. And yours?" He makes eye contact with the bartender and motions to put their drinks on his tab.

"I'm Bunny. This is Charley." She motions to the lovely woman beside her. She's dainty and mischievous, leaning her head against Bunny's shoulder.

"Nice to meet you, Henri," she coos. He smiles and gives her offered hand a light shake while searching the room behind them.

"Looking for someone?" Bunny askes with yet another giggle. He looks back at her. Her smiling eyes and round cheeks are lovely. A day ago, or even that morning, he would've been interested. Maybe even asked to take her out and show her the town. He enjoyed the playful way giggles followed her words, like vocal punctuation. But her pretty face and playful giggles meant only one thing to him. He was close to his angel.

"I am, in fact. You were with someone earlier today. It seems you caught my name then disappeared into thin air. Did she happen to go with you?"

"She did," Bunny says slyly. "Would you like to accompany us to our table? Looks like we have more drinks than hands." Henri's mood lifts with every word she says. He looks up to Jo in the stage lights, who's looking down with a grin, nodding his head.

"I would love to." With drinks in hand, Henri follows his new friends to a table in the back of the bar. His angel is sitting in the booth with two women, beaming. Her full lips spread wide in an amazing smile. She looks up, acknowledging her friends' return from the bar. Then her eyes settle on him. Her laughter stops, her smile softens, and the music fades. She's suspended in that same dreamlike gold dust shimmer as she had been earlier today. She blinks and looks down at her drink then back at him with dazzling eyes.

"We meet again, *cherie*," he says with all the charm he can muster while battling the lump in his throat.

***

Bridgette looks up as Bunny approaches the table. Behind her, with an irresistible smile and a dreamy look in his eye, stands Henri. He's carrying two drinks. One is Bridgette's. "We meet again, *cherie*." His smooth French said in a deep Southern voice seems to touch her skin. "This is fortuitous." He hands her a drink. Her fingers brush his with a tingle. Their eyes meet. He stands, waiting for an invitation to join.

"Henri?" Trixie exclaims. "I knew you looked familiar. Remember me? Trixie?" Bridgette watches as Henri narrows his eyes, searching for recognition. "We went to school together. Well, briefly. I guess until you disappeared to wherever you went. We were in algebra. I think. I guess I was in algebra. You showed up sometimes." He raises an eyebrow and shakes his head slowly, looking puzzled. "Ooh. They called me Bea then. That's my muggle name." She laughs at herself and sucks at her straw, draining the contents of her drink. Then, plucking it out, she drops it into her fresh beverage. "This is how I keep track," she says to the table. "Once I have too many straws it's time to order water."

Bridgette is watching Henri as recognition dawns. He smiles broadly. "Ah, Bea. I do remember. You've changed."

"You haven't," she tells him. "Look the same." She eyes him up and down. "Dress better, I suppose. No more angsty skater punk or whatever you were going for." She turns to Bridgette, as though he's not there. "He's a nice guy. A little spoiled, if I remember. But he was always nice to me."

"Now, Trixie, none of us were at that school based on merit," he teases.

"You're right," she quips back. "But I said spoiled, not rich."

"Touché," he says, placing his hand on an empty chair. "May I?" he asks, looking to Bridgette with a glint in his dark soulful eyes, then to Lilian.

"Sure thing, man," Lilian responds, sliding closer to Bridgette to make room for his chair. "I'm Lilian. Pretty sure we run in the same circles."

"Do we?" he asks, setting his drink on the table. A piece of his perfect jet hair falls out of place, over his eye. He brushes it back with a quick swipe of his hand. His gold watch glints in the light from the stage.

"Yeah. You ever go to the Backdoor?"

"I've been there a time or two," he answers, but his eyes are on Bridgette. She's looking back at him. His skin looks so smooth. She longs to reach across the table and touch it. To confirm that he's there in the flesh, not some New Orleans ghost wandering the streets, toying with tourists.

"Now, you have me at a disadvantage," he says to Bridgette, ignoring everyone at the table. Lilian looks at her with a sneer and wide eyes as if to say, *Is this guy for real?* "May I have your name?"

The way he speaks seems to be from another era. Bridgette wonders again at his realness. But there is something about him that she can't resist. He's been in the back of her mind since that "moment" they shared earlier that day. She's been searching the crowds all night with a secret hope that he'd appear. And here he is at her table, asking for her name.

"I'm Bridgette," she says, her name sounding foreign on her tongue. A smile plays at the corner of his mouth. She shifts under his gaze. To be watched on stage was one thing. To be sitting up close and in person, the focus of his penetrating stare, was a whole new kind of discomfort.

"I'm pleased to meet you, Bridgette. I had hoped to introduce myself this afternoon, but you vanished."

"I had somewhere to be," she told him. Their words, though mundane, are charged with electricity. She's anxious to be closer to him, to know more.

"Geeze, enchanted moment over here," Lilian sneers. "Let me get out of your way." She laughs and picks up her chair and carries it to the other side of the table. Henri slides his closer to Bridgette without a word of thanks. He's near enough for her to smell his cologne. It's light and tropical, almost floral, feminine, but it's irresistible and masculine at the same time. She breathes it in and closes her eyes.

"Would you believe me if I told you I'd been searching all night for you?" His words are soft and slow. She opens her eyes to him, her cheeks warm with his admiration.

"I've been keeping my eye out for you too," she whispers. A tiny smile plays at the corner of his mouth again. His eyes crinkle.

"That's music to my ears, *cher*." He rests one elbow on the tabletop and turns in her direction, cutting off the rest of her group. She eyes Bunny over his shoulder. Bunny looks back with one eyebrow raised. Bridgette responds with a flutter of lashes and a smile. A subtle cue that everything is okay. Bunny nods and returns her attention to the group's conversation. "What brings you to New Orleans? Business or pleasure?" he asks then takes a sip of his drink. "I pity the poor fellow that comes for business."

"Both actually." She smiles.

"Ah, I'm intrigued." The cadence of his speech is like honey, slow and smooth.

"I'm a burlesque dancer. I'm here to perform tomorrow night with them." She nods toward the group of women casually chatting. Bridgette knows their chat is a cover. They're all tuned into her exchange with the enigmatic Henri. The women are reading his body language, assessing his intentions, watching her face for any sign of distress. Her heart warms at the thought of the unspoken bond between them, and their desire to protect and defend one another. She eyes his response to her statement about burlesque. Some men can't handle it. Some are turned on. Some are genuinely interested.

"You know, I've lived here my entire life and never seen a burlesque show."

"Really?" Bridgette asks. Not surprised. Burlesque is sort of underground art.

"Nope. It's music that gets me. Like my friend up there." He gestures to the man on stage. She's suddenly aware of the music again. "Jo is amazing. So much talent in one man. It seems unfair to the rest of us." He looks away from her for the first time to watch as Jo plays his guitar and hums into the mic.

"Do you play?" she asks, watching him be taken away by the sound.

"Hmm?" He turns back, her question registering slowly. "Yeah. But not like that. So, where are you from?"

"Chicago."

"How long are you here?"

"For the weekend." She notes an almost imperceptible twitch to his eye.

"That's a shame," he says, bringing his drink to his lips. "You need at least two weeks to fully appreciate this town." He takes a long drink. "A lifetime to see it all."

"I believe it. I used to come with my grandparents all the time as a kid. But I've never seen the nightlife."

"Well, that's the best part."

Bridgette cringes at the thought of the nightlife she recently experienced. The drunk men shouting from the balconies at every female who walked past. She was shocked to see how many would expose their breasts for nothing more than their slovenly cheers.

Henri knits his brow with a squint and a tilt of his head. Then he looks out the window. "I'm not talking about what's out there." He shakes his head with a grimace. "I'm talking about in here." He smiles. "Places like the Backdoor. The places *we* go." He pats his chest and gestures to Lilian and the others. Lowering his voice, he leans closer to Bridgette. His scent is almost hypnotizing. "The secret places," he says with a wink, brushing the errant strand from his eye again.

"I like secret places," she says with blatant innuendo.

"I'd love to show you some of them." Their stare is intense. Bridgette bites her bottom lip and bats her lashes. She reaches for her drink and sips slowly. Under the table she uncrosses and crosses her legs, leaning toward him.

***

Bridgette's foot brushes his leg as she leans closer. A smile plays on her luscious lips. Henri watches shamelessly as she toys with her straw. He shifts in his seat as his groin stirs. "What would you like to see?" he asks as slow and smooth as he can manage. *She's fucking perfect.* Resting one hand on his knee, he leans back with his drink in the other. "Name it, we'll go."

She raises her eyebrow and leans back herself. "Right now?" She uncrosses her legs, her cutoffs creeping up her thighs, exposing her tattoo completely, a burst of colorful flowers, feathers, and pearls. His fingers itch to trace the lines of it, to run farther up under the frayed denim. She rests one hand on her stomach, playing with the fringe of her shirt. She follows his gaze and laughs. "I'm not going anywhere with you." He winces at the sound of her words. "Not tonight anyway." More laughter.

"No?"

"Oh no," she teases.

"How about tomorrow morning? Can I take you to breakfast?" he asks, trying to keep his tone and his body language calm and cool.

"Maybe." She turns away from him. "Bunny. When does Mike get in tomorrow?"

"He said he'd be at the hotel by noon," she answers from behind Henri. He's elated at the thought. He knows exactly where to take her.

"How about brunch?" he asks, swirling the ice in his empty glass. "Then, maybe I can show you a few of my favorite places."

"I'd like that." She smiles, finishing her drink, crossing her legs again. His gaze follows the movement and lands where denim and warm tan skin meet as her shorts creep higher still. A gateway to heaven, no doubt. "Where are you taking me?"

Anywhere you want to go, he thinks as he imagines what he would do with those thighs. He clears his throat. "Have you been to the Court of Two Sisters?"

"I think I read about it at the hotel earlier. It's not far from me. I can meet you there."

"Perfect." They fall silent. Henri takes in the movement of her chest as her breath seems to increase. He watches the subtle grace as she brings her straw to her lips again. The busy way she fiddles with the fringe of her shirt. She's delightfully exposed. It's torture to not see more. But he can see more if he'd like for the price of a ticket to the show. "So, where's the show?" he asks, trying for mild curiosity.

"Lilian," Bridgette calls behind him. He regrets losing her attention. "We're at the Backdoor tomorrow night, right?"

"Yep. Doors at eight-thirty. Show's at nine. We go on about ten." She's moved her chair to insert herself into their conversation. Henri hides his disappointment with a tight smile. "Interesting you went to school with Trixie."

"I did," he answers with some irritation.

"She said you left abruptly. Why?" Lilian asks. Was it genuine curiosity or an accusation of some sort?

"I had my reasons," he says, turning toward her. His face is warming as he fights the unpleasant words that play on his tongue. "It was a family matter if you must know." It wasn't a lie, not really, but it wasn't the kind of thing you talked about moments after meeting the woman of your dreams.

"Huh." She eyes him skeptically, then looks at Bridgette, and back to him. "I think we're calling it a night pretty soon. Are you and Bunny all right to get back to your hotel?" Henri hears the unspoken words. This is code for *Do we need to get you out of here away from this unsavory man?* He can read the room, and being no fool, he knows what his next move should be. As much as he wants to stay and talk the night away, getting to know everything there is to know about Bridgette, he knows that her ladies in waiting are not going to let her out of their sight.

He looks from Lilian to Bridgette. Taking in the lovely curve of her cheek, the sweet way her mouth smiles even relaxed, it's the opposite of resting bitch face. Or in Lilian's case, active bitch face. Glancing at his watch, he smiles at them both. "I should be getting on my way as well. How should I reach you for brunch?" he asks Bridgette. They exchange numbers. Then, standing, he looks down at her with a smile. "Until tomorrow, *cher*." He nods to the rest of her friends. They call their good-byes in unison.

He leaves the club with mixed emotions. His search had been successful. Not only had he met her and learned her name, but he was going to see her again. Alone. *Thank god for that. How's a man supposed to get to know a woman in a situation like that?* Then there was Trixie. Or Bea. Her presence had been an unwelcome surprise that brought with it his past.

His story fit so uncomfortably well in the tiny box he built for it in his psyche. Guilt weighs heavy on his otherwise happy heart as he walks through the busy street. The hot and heavy air smells of rain on its way.

Chapter 4

"What did you think of Henri?" Bridgette asks as she combs her hair. She's sitting beside Bunny on the couch in their hotel room. It's late morning. The city below them is already bustling with people.

"Hmm. It's hard to say. I mean, he pretty much ignored everyone at the table from the moment he laid eyes on you. The way he sat down all possessive like was a bit unnerving. Lilian called him an arrogant fuck."

"Yeah. But I kinda liked it. I liked his confidence."

"You say confidence, we say arrogance. The difference is in the perception, I suppose."

"He's handsome. And god, Bunny, he smelled so good. Like delicious even."

"I didn't notice. Guess I'll have to smell him next time I see him."

"Please don't."

"Come on, I want to smell the delicious man too."

"You'll have your own to smell soon enough." Bridgette looks at the clock on the desk. It's ten-thirty. "Mike should be landing soon." She stands and looks in the mirror. Her knee-length, pale green sundress fits snugly on her waist and floats over her hips down to her knees. "How do I look?"

"Beautiful, *cher*," Bunny teases with her poor attempt at Henri's accent. Bridgette rolls her eyes.

"Shut up. I'm leaving."

"Okay. You sure you don't want me to walk along? I'm not doing anything here, only waiting for Mike."

"I'll be all right. It's only a few blocks away. Thanks though."

"Call if you need us to come rescue you."

"We both know you won't be answering your phone as soon as Mike gets here."

"Not true. I can answer my phone with a dick in me." She laughs.

"Please don't."

"I'm beginning to think you're embarrassed of me." More laughter.

"I'm embarrassed for you, Bunny. Get it together."

"Ha. Never." She stands and crosses to the window. "I'm going to sip coffee and watch people. Have fun with your handsome voodoo man."

"I will. Not sure when I'll be back," she says, gathering her things into a small purse. "I'm gonna call before I come up for sure."

"Whatever. We'll be decent. I promise. Have fun."

"Love you."

"Love you too."

Bridgette steps into the elevator, more excited than she can remember being for a brunch date. Checking her reflection in the mirrored door, she gives herself a pep talk. *He doesn't stand a chance.* She bites her lip and kisses the air, then grins at the thought of finally touching his face. Of getting closer than she should and breathing in deeply that irresistible scent. The doors slide open and she exits into the richly colored lobby, which smells of coffee and pastries. A handful of sleepy people pass by. A doorman smiles and greets her, opening the door. Outside, the air is thick and damp, the sky overcast. People are milling about with frequent glances to the heavens. Their silent prayers for the bad weather to hold off one more day so they can continue their vacations. Bridgette walks along, oblivious to their worries, and enjoys the warm breeze playing at the hem of her dress.

Four blocks later, she arrives at the Court of Two Sisters. The deep green double doors greet her with a large half-circle window above. It reminds her of the rising sun. Through the door, she's transported, yet again, back in time. What should be a vestibule is an alleyway with stones worn smooth by generations of foot traffic. The walls are exposed brick with an iron gate on display. A sign beside it says it's The Charm Gate given to the two sisters by Queen Isabella II of Spain. It claims to have been blessed with magic powers promising love and good fortune to those who touch it. Bridgette smiles as she runs her fingers along the cold iron. She laughs to herself. *Everything in the city has a story.*

"We keep meeting like this." Henri speaks soft and close to her ear from behind her. She jumps. Normally, behavior like this would be unacceptable. Personal boundaries are important to her. But, as his scent envelops her, she can't find a reason to complain.

"Are you referring to the way you creep up on me when I'm not looking?" she asks without facing him, all too aware of his nearness.

"Not quite," he says, leaning against the wall beside the Charm Gate. He's dressed in a white linen shirt that could stand to lose a button or two. Bridgette imagines loosening them one at a time, gaining access to his smooth chest. His casual gray slacks are pressed but well worn. He crosses one polished shoe over the other and crosses his arms over his chest. "I'm referring to you daydreaming in public. What are those dreams I wonder." He smiles with a crinkle at the edge of his eyes.

"Wouldn't you like to know." She smiles back. "This place is lovely."

"Wait 'til you see the courtyard." He stands straight and offers his arm to walk with her. Bridgette slips her hand comfortably above his elbow. His skin is warm and smooth under the light fabric. She holds on softly as he leads the way down the indoor alleyway into a pink corridor. It smells wet, almost musty. This is a city that celebrates its decay instead of hiding it. At times it seems its inhabitants revel in it.

A hostess leads them through a bright white dining room into a courtyard. Wisteria branches spread out above tables dressed with white linens. Small birds flit in and out overhead. A three-piece brass band plays in the corner. Bubbling in the center of it all is a four-tier fountain. Against a wall to the back of the courtyard is a statue of two young women. One's arm is draped over the other's shoulder. They stand amongst tropical plants, their breasts exposed in natural comfort. Their table is right beside the sculpture. Bridgette settles into her seat, wishing she hadn't chosen to leave her camera at home. She considers using her phone to snap a few quick pictures then looks at Henri and forgets everything except his handsome face.

"I thought you might like that," Henri says, nodding toward the statue.

"Why's that?" Bridgette asks with genuine curiosity.

"Well, as a burlesque dancer, I assumed you would appreciate the female form on display as it is."

"You were right. I love it." She looks around, taking in the courtyard from her new angle. "What I wouldn't do to have my camera with me."

"You're a photographer?" he asks, leaning on the table.

"I'm more into design work. But yeah. I do some photography too. They go hand in hand, really."

"I guess I thought you were a full-time performer."

"It's a common misconception. Burlesque costs more money than it makes." She shrugs. "It's a labor of love." Their server floats over to fill their coffee cups. The bittersweet roast chicory aroma fills her nose. Her mouth waters instantly. She sips, watching over the rim of her cup as Henri fills his with enough sugar and cream to bake a cake. He orders mimosas for them both.

"Art rarely pays anything," he states, "unless it's marketed properly. Then, the age-old question arises, is it still art? Once it's marketed, that is."

"What do you mean?"

"Art created for profit's sake seems to lose its mystery. Its spark. Jo gets it. He refused to step foot in the studio for years for that exact reason."

"Is that what you do?"

"Some of what I do."

"I'm curious. You already know a lot about me. All I know is that you were spoiled, went to a private school, and you like music and voodoo?"

"Voodoo?" He smiles and laughs.

"Well, you were in the shop, you knew about Papa Legba."

"Everyone here knows about Papa Legba. I was in the shop for Jo. Glad I was too." He stares across the table holding her gaze. "I was spoiled, and I do love music. But there's more to me than that. What would you like to know?"

"How do you make your living?"

"That's an interesting question."

"How so?"

"My living was made for me." He leans on his elbows, fingers clasped above his empty plate. "My family has been here for centuries. They started with sugar cane then moved into developing and government. There isn't a law passed or ground broken without the name Dauphine attached."

"Should I be impressed?" She raises her eyebrow, thinking of how her father chased status like Henri's her entire life. How his pursuit of money and success had broken her family apart. Nothing was ever good enough, including her and her mom.

"Hear me out," he says, sitting up and spreading his hands open in a display of honesty. "It seems like bragging, but it's fact. You'll learn eventually. No sense in hiding it. I could buy and sell this place a dozen times over and make no difference to my bottom line."

"Wow. Your modesty is impressive," she huffs, liking him better as the mysterious voodoo man of few words.

"My apologies, *cher*." He sits back, one hand on his coffee cup. "I didn't mean to be boastful."

"You might be the most boastful person I've ever met." She sips her coffee again, remembering her father preening in the mirror as he talked about his next big venture, how great it was going to be, how great *he* was going to be. She wishes, briefly, she was back at the hotel people watching with Bunny.

"Can we start over?" Their server arrives, pouring mimosas at the table and disappearing. Bridgette watches him skeptically. His expression gives his silent plea. He has to be more than a pretty face and charming voice. Looking at him, she remembers why she agreed to meet him. It wasn't his mysterious air or his handsome face. There was something genuine about him. His eyes conveyed emotion even when he tried to hide it. For that alone, he deserved a chance.

"Okay. But your money won't impress me." She offers a small smile.

"I don't know." He chuckles. "I feel like I could impress you with my money."

"Money makes it easy. What are you without it?"

He blinks and sits silently looking from her to the fountain, then to his coffee. "That's a hell of a question. Shall we eat while I suffer this existential dilemma you've presented me with?"

She bites her cheek and studies him, sorry for the shift in his demeanor. Her stomach growls. "Sure thing," she responds with another gentle smile of encouragement.

***

Way to go, idiot. Henri fills his plate with some of the most sumptuous brunch foods in New Orleans, wondering if he can regain lost ground. The smells of sweet and savory mingle delightfully in the air. But they are lost on him. He's watching as Bridgette takes a bit of everything from the buffet. She glides along as though he isn't there. Her skirt brushes his leg as she passes on her way to their table. He hurries to follow her. No sense in taking more than he'll eat. Considering his appetite is for something else altogether. *How to impress her?* He watches the way her hips sway a few steps ahead of him.

She's enjoying the food before he joins her. "This is amazing," she says from behind her napkin. "I can't decide which I like more." With a long drink from her mimosa, she turns her attention back to her food.

"Glad you like it." He smiles, enjoying the shameless way she's devouring her food. "Would you say you're impressed?" She snorts. The server is back refilling the bottomless mimosas.

"Yeah. By the chef. You're going to have to try harder."

He pokes at his plate, sips at his mimosa, and watches her. She's beautiful in her sundress, pale green spaghetti straps hanging loosely on her shoulders. A slight turn or bend in the right direction reveals a glimpse of her pert, dainty breast. Oblivious to her charms, she continues to enjoy her hearty breakfast.

"Ask me anything," he tells her with an unintentional hint of desperation. "Anything you want to know."

She looks up from her plate, big brown eyes shining. "What's your family like?"

"They're perfect." He sighs. "My brothers are wildly successful. One in business, one in law. They have beautiful wives from good Southern families. They each have a boy and girl. My sister is a perfect Southern belle who married into a family of high standing with two beautiful, precocious daughters. My parents are incredibly proud of them all." She lays her fork on her plate and eyes him with her mimosa in hand.

"What about you?"

"Well, they love me," he says, regretting the pity in her eyes. "I'm Mama's sweet boy," he says with a derisive laugh. She tilts her head and looks away. *What the fuck, man? You're losing her.* "But

I'm the youngest. They didn't have a lot planned for me. Can't really say I'm a disappointment. How about you?"

"I'm an only child. Raised by my grandparents mostly. My folks were divorced and busy starting their lives over again. I ended up with my grandparents a lot. They were good to me. Spoiled me some. Mostly with love and attention." She smiles.

"To be spoiled with love isn't possible."

She looks at him with curiosity in her eyes, and is it pity? "I've heard that too." She finishes her mimosa in time for the server to refill it. "I always dreamed of having a brother or sister though."

"It's overrated." He waves a hand in the air, draining his mimosa. He remembers the constant teasing from his older brothers, the comparisons from his parents. His sister had always been sweet. Though she wasn't given an option to be any other way.

Bridgette's cheeks are coloring from their bottomless beverage. She looks away and drinks more, her discomfort obvious. She clears her throat. "What was Trixie like in school?"

Henri is grateful for the change in subject. He does his best to remember the awkward girl from so many years before. "To be honest, I don't remember her much. I wouldn't have known her if she hadn't said anything." He sits up straighter. "She was always reading and talking about muggles and what not. Big Harry Potter fan. And anime, I think. She would talk about the most obscure things. People weren't particularly kind to her."

"But you were," she says, picking up her fork.

"Was I?" he asks, hoping that he still had a chance to redeem himself.

"She said you always had a smile for her."

"I've got a great smile. I like to share it with the world," he says, teasing.

"You do," she agrees. "So, where'd you disappear to?"

"I'm sorry." He's confused. "I didn't realize I'd gone anywhere."

"Not now. In school. Trixie said you disappeared. Where'd you go?"

His heart stings from the question. Memories of pain and anguish too deep to share. She presses her lips together and watches him with a quizzical look. He downs his drink and shifts in his seat, placing a napkin over his plate. What little appetite he had is gone.

"You cut right to things, don't you?" He fights the lump in his throat. It pushes with years of self-loathing and pain. "I was sent away. To my great-grandmother in Japan," he answers with a crack in his voice. "My parents thought it would be best." She reaches for her water, looking away from him to her plate then somewhere in the distance.

"I'm sorry," she says softly.

"Don't be." He reaches for his water. "I was getting into a lot of trouble. My parents felt they had no control over me," he tells her, hoping it is enough. Though his past was unavoidable, he had hoped to enjoy his brief time with the lovely woman without revealing it. Their plates are taken away. He leans on his elbows, resting his chin on his clasped hands. "Now, where would you like to go?"

Chapter 5

"What do you think?" he asks as they walk along the riverfront. Its murky waters ripple without the sparkle of sunshine. Henri has become her tour guide. All his charm has returned and its multiplied by his love for the city. It's in the sweet way his eyes crinkle when he smiles at a passerby. Or in the way he points out the smallest details of architecture and design. More than once, he holds fast to her elbow to listen to a street musician. Then, he leaves a generous offering before they are on their way.

"It's impressive… Bigger than I remember," she says, trying to tame her hair and dress as the heavy breeze lifts them. He steps behind her, dangerously close. One shift of her body and he could wrap her in his arms. She could lean into him and feel the warmth she knows is there, smell the scent that she has already grown so fond of. But then what? Once she breaks that barrier there's no turning back. If she falls into his arms here on the riverfront, she'll keep falling until she's drowning in his touch. Then she'll lose herself like her mother had for every handsome man with a bank account. Better to keep a safe distance and keep moving. "You know what else I remember?" she asks over her shoulder, taking a step away from him.

"What's that?" He follows one step behind, barely out of reach.

"The streetcars. I loved them so much as a kid. Not sure if my grandparents did. But they would always take me for at least one ride around town. I loved the sound of them the most, I think, and the way the windows were open. It always seemed so exotic and dangerous." She laughs. Henri hurries to walk beside her.

"We can go now if you want," he offers. "There's a stop right up there." He points away from the river toward the French market.

"Oh yes. I would love that." Her excitement is impossible to hide.

"Well, let's go then."

There are only a few people waiting on the curb when they arrive. Shortly after the streetcar rattles to a stop. Dozens of people step off the back while they are welcomed aboard by a gruff old man. Henri offers his hand as she steps up. It has all the warmth she expects. She holds it as he boards behind her, leading him to an empty bench in the back. Her heart is floating, full of happy memories as she sits next to the window. With his hand still in hers, he settles beside her. She looks out at the yellowing gray sky as more people hurry up to board. What started as only a few are now twenty or more. Everyone is comfortably seated as the streetcar shakes back to life with a jolt. Bridgette can feel the ridiculous grin on her face. She watches the city slip by slowly as the car clatters down the road.

"We can take this all the way to the Garden District," Henri says, his hand lying open on his knee, hers still resting there.

"That would be amazing. We used to go there and walk around to look at all the houses. Pretty sure that was my grandparents' favorite part." His eyes sparkle as a grin creeps across his face. Bridgette is at once embarrassed. "Wait. Don't even tell me." She pulls her hand away and waves it in the air. "You probably grew up in one." She sighs, cheeks red, and looks out the window.

"I grew up out of town," he says, slow and smooth. "But…I do own a modest place there now."

"It would be the first thing about you that is."

"It's a small cottage off Magazine. My family doesn't like the city. They prefer the country or the suburbs. I can't get enough of everything New Orleans." The car stops suddenly, and Bridgette braces herself with one hand on the window and the other on his knee. The doors open and more people enter. A large man stands directly beside their seat, forcing Henri to slide farther in. Their bodies press together, her hand stays on his knee.

"It's getting tight in here." He laughs, eyes darting around the car as it fills even more.

"It is," she agrees, not able to comfortably move her hand.

"Sorry." He gives her a bashful smile.

"It's okay, really." She pats his knee. His hand rests on hers, fingers curling around it. Something shifts. His nearness is undeniable. They had been politely avoiding contact all day. But here on the streetcar with scores of people around, it's no longer possible. Their hips, their shoulders, their thighs are pressed together by the weight of strangers. "This is awkward," she huffs. Though she wants more than anything to kiss him, to turn her body to him so he can take her in his arms.

"We can get off anytime. But they are all this full," he says gently.

"Are we almost to Magazine? I wouldn't mind seeing your little cottage."

"Three more stops," he replies.

"You think we'll make it? If this car takes any more people, I'll be in your lap."

"I can think of worse things." He smiles and squeezes her hand.

Bridgette's silent as they barrel onto the next stop. The sweet scent of jasmine drifts through the open window. She leans into Henri with a subtle message. Flipping her hand up, their palms meet. He laces his fingers through hers and lifts her hand to his chest, grazing her knuckles with a light kiss. Something carnal stirs in her as his lips stay delicate against her skin.

She feels her cheeks blaze from desire.

***

"Well, here it is," Henri says with a nervous chuckle as they stroll along the uneven sidewalk. His two-story raised cottage sits not far from where they stop, deep green with white columns and shutters. A sprawling live oak grows on the other side of a wrought-iron fence. She drops his hand, which she had been holding since the streetcar. He fights his urge to get it back and kiss it one thousand times more.

"This is modest?" She turns to look back at him. Both of her hands rest on the gate.

"Compared to a lot of these houses, yes." He nods while swiping at his hair. "Do you want to see inside?" She smiles with her beautiful tempting lips. It takes all of him to not press her against the gate and taste them.

"I do, actually. It's embarrassing to say it, but it's kind of a dream come true."

"Don't be embarrassed. It was my dream too. These houses have such a charm about them." He steps beside her to unlock the gate and swing it in. "After you." He gestures. She passes through with a child-like expression of wonder on her beautiful face. He locks the gate and follows her quickly up the stairs.

"I love the view from here," she breathes, looking out across the street.

"Me too," Henri murmurs, his eyes on her, especially the way her dress hugs her curves.

She catches him staring. A smile spreads across her face. She tosses her hair over her shoulder and rolls her eyes. "Oh please."

"All right, all right." He laughs at himself. There's a familiar barking and scratching at the other side of the door.

"You have a dog?" she asks, voice rising with each word. Henri unlocks the door, grins, and pushes it open. Bones rushes out to meet them. His whole butt is wagging as he jumps to reach Henri's hands. "Oh my god. He's so cute. Come here you." She kneels and calls him over.

"That dog is not cute," he responds, shaking his head.

"But he's so sweet."

"I'll give him that. He's got character." The medium-size mutt is lapping at her chin, butting his big ugly head into her breast.

"What's his name?" She's scratching his ears and cooing.

"Bones. At least that's what I call him. I found him one day digging through my trash. He was bone thin and smelled like rot. Hence the name." His tongue lolls out of his goofy crooked face as he rolls on his back for tummy scratches. *Lucky bastard,* Henri thinks, watching as he loses her to the dog.

"Oh Bones, you lucky boy, you. You're so fat and fluffy now. What a good boy." Her absolute joy is the purest thing he's ever seen.

"Come on, Bonesy. Inside." He snaps his fingers. Bones jumps up and runs into the house.

"What a good boy," she calls after him, grinning.

"He really is. Keeps me company anyway." He offers his hand. She takes it and stands, dusting the fur off her dress.

"Thanks. Though I'm sure you have no problem finding company."

"I do okay." He steps aside holding the door wide. "My lady." He motions for her to enter before him.

***

Inside, it smells of floor polish and old wood. The entryway is split with a hall on one side and a curving stairway on the other. At Bridgette's feet, black and white tiles are laid in an intricate art deco pattern. She sighs with delight, taking in every detail. To her right is the parlor, its furnishings luxurious and modern. An oversize piece of brightly colored Haitian art hangs over the mantel of the fireplace. Bridgette's artist's eye appreciates the room's neutral tones with pops of color picked up from the painting. A bright pink throw pillow here. A neon green vase there. The oriental rug pulls it together with the same colors, only muted. Tropical plants flourish in front of every window. The interior shutters, the same wood as the floors, are open to let in light. "Did you do that?" she asks, pointing to the room.

"That depends on what that is." He looks in the direction she's pointing. He's standing close again. Close enough that she can feel his energy, smell his haunting scent.

"The decorating. It's smart and beautifully done. I'm impressed." She finds more to love about the room the longer she looks.

"Damn. I wish it had been me. I found the painting and had a friend do the rest."

"A friend?" she asks, wondering who she was, ashamed of the twinge of jealousy she felt.

"Yes, a close friend of mine is in interior design. She has a boutique down on Magazine. Her thing is pairing the beauty of antiques with the function and comfort of modern design. She does great work. Did the whole house. It wasn't in the best shape when I bought it. You want to see the rest?" Bones runs up and down the halls, claws clicking on the tile. "I think he's hungry. Come on, I'll show you the kitchen."

Not surprised after seeing the parlor, the entire place is decorated beautifully. Even the more casual living room with its plush couches and dark drapes pulled shut against the daylight.

"Do you smoke?" he asks, sitting on one of the couches.

"Smoke what?" Bridgette asks.

"Smoke?" he says again, pulling a drawer open from under the coffee table. Bridgette sits beside him, sinking into the cloudlike couch. The contents of the drawer a regular stoner's kit set out on a tray. The pungent, skunky smell rises as he opens a jar.

"I do," she answers, pleased by the offer. Though drinking wasn't her thing, she'd be the first to admit to having a vice. He packs a bowl and hands it to her with a lighter. She lights it and inhales deeply.

"Careful, it's some pretty strong stuff." She breathes in the familiar taste and holds it, appreciating the flavor. Her exhale, however, is not smooth. A coughing fit erupts in her chest to the point that her eyes water and her stomach hurts. It's loud and embarrassing. Henri lays his hand on her back. "Sorry, I should have warned you right away." She waves her hand in the air and closes her eyes. The high is instant.

"It's okay," she squeaks. "Can I have some water?" He hurries to the small wet bar in the corner and grabs a bottle of water from a mini-fridge. "Thank you. I'm okay, really. Wasn't expecting that." She chuckles and takes a small sip. She feels as though she's sinking even farther into the couch. Her dress and undergarments are suddenly tight and uncomfortable, the seams scratching at her skin. "Fuck," she mutters, shifting for comfort. "That was strong."

"Yeah," he agrees, lighting the bowl for himself. After a couple hits, he lays it down on the tray and sits back. "We need some music." He reaches for a remote and pushes a button that opens a pair of drapes, revealing a large smart TV. The unexpected sound of accordion music fills the air. It's half tango and half carnival. The joyful rhythm tickles her and makes her want to dance.

"This is nice." She closes her eyes to watch the colors play behind her lids.

"Yeah," he responds, shifting. She opens her eyes and turns to see him watching her.

"Stop."

"Stop what?"

"Stop watching me. It's weird."

"Sorry. You're…"

"High as fuck and not comfortable with you staring at me."

"You're right." He shifts back to watch the ceiling. Bridgette does the same. The pressed tin tiles, some fourteen feet above, are painted black. "Sorry," he says to the ceiling. Time passes.

"What are we listening to?" she asks with genuine curiosity.

"It's Parisian accordion. I found a record once in an old resale shop and fell in love." His fingers dance in the air to the playful sound.

"I like it." She shifts, sinking farther into the plush sofa. The song ends with a crescendo. Then silence. A new song begins, sexy and slow. A woman sings in French. The space of one cushion separates her from Henri. Bridgette is painfully aware of her skin and her desire for it to be bare and touched. Her hand rests on her stomach. His at his side. She could reach out and touch it. Her fingers could run up the length of his arm. They itch to do it.

"So, where'd Bones go?" she asks instead.

"I don't know," he says and clicks his teeth. The mutt comes running into the room and bounces on the couch between them. He licks Henri's face and wags his tail furiously. "Hey, buddy," he greets and scratches the dog's head. Bridgette's heart swells as she watches the affectionate show. Their eyes meet. He's smiling the bright smile that reaches his eyes, that she's come to adore.

"So, what's upstairs?" she asks, knowing the answer. His smile stays put as his lips take a more sensual turn.

"My studio, my bedroom, and a bathroom. The rest is unfinished. I use it for storage mostly." Bones has settled his head on Henri's lap. Henri's hand rests on his back.

"What's in your studio?"

"Mostly sound equipment, instruments, and whatnot."

"I'd like to see it," she says, knowing that a walk up the stairs could lead to more than checking out his studio.

"Yeah? Okay." He stands, offering his hand to her. She takes it and stands too. "Follow me."

The music from the back room fades as they ascend the stairs. The air is warmer and smells of dust. To the right, the door is open to a bedroom as luxurious as the rest of the house. Bridgette imagines what the pillows would feel like piled under her head with Henri beside her.

The shutters are open, lighting the room with natural dreamy light. "That's my room," he says, nodding toward the open door. Then, pushing the door directly across from it, he stands aside. "Here's my studio." There are no shutters in the room, no windows even. "It's soundproof. Bricked up the windows and covered them." In one corner there's a control center with soundboard and computers. The walls are covered with a variety of mounted instruments. Drums of various styles and sizes line the floor.

"Do you play all of these?" She gestures to the wall of instruments.

Henri watches as she walks along the wall, eyeing each instrument. She's a refreshing sight in his favorite room. It's large enough to fit several musicians and their equipment; at times it does. But most often he's here alone, recording, mixing, making music that no one will ever hear.

"I dabble in them all, but I prefer the guitar."

"Hmm," she murmurs. "What's that?" She points to his theremin. It's set on a stand looking like something from a science fiction movie.

"That is a theremin," he states. She tilts her head and looks unamused.

"What's a theremin?"

"It's pretty cool. Imagine the spooky alien music from old movies." She stares blankly. "Here, listen." He flips it on, holding his hands in place, one above the curved horizontal bar, the other beside the straight vertical one. An eerie tone emits into the air. Bridgette's eyes widen, and a smile breaks across her face.

"That's fucking amazing." She laughs. "Can I try?"

"Sure." He steps back and watches as she manipulates the sound with her hands. With the natural rhythm of a dancer, she's able to make a strange melody with the theremin. Joy lights her face.

"This is so cool. I'd love to hoop to this." She wiggles her hips to her beat, her body moving an imaginary hula hoop in the air. "I could be an alien. My hoop could be my spaceship. This is so cool."

"Glad you like it." He pauses. "Would you say you're impressed?"

"Yeah. I am. Looks like you did it."

"Since that was a gift, you could say I managed to impress you without money. Right?"

"Looks like." She laughs and continues to play with the theremin.

"Would you like to see the view from the porch up here?"

"I would." She beams and plays a few more notes on the instrument with a giggle. "I love that thing."

"It's right out here." He directs her back into the hallway and out through the large wooden door. Potted plants line either side of the porch. Jasmine grows over the railings. The smell is heavenly. "This is one of my favorite spots."

"I can see why. I think I might sleep out here," she says with a deep breath.

"Sometimes I do when the weather's perfect." She eyes the luxe, oversize chaise lounge. "Try it out," he says with an indulgent smile. "It's as comfortable as it looks."

Henri watches as she sits on its plush cushions looking out over the street. Her face is serene, her shapely thighs hidden under a thin layer of green. He aches to see them on display as they were the night before. Dainty feet lay bare on the chaise with toes painted bright, lipstick red. As he brushes his hair out of his eyes, Bones trots out and jumps onto her lap. "Get down," Henri calls, snapping his fingers. "Sorry. He's not great with boundaries." He laughs. "A crazy mutt, like me. Probably why I took to him so easily."

"So now you're a mutt?" she asks with a flip of her hair.

"Well, yeah." He gestures at his face. "I ain't no pure breed."

"That's right, you did say your great-grandma was from Japan. I guess it didn't register. But your DNA is what makes your hair so perfect." She grins. "It's one of the first things I noticed about you." Her laugh is a light and beautiful sound.

"Yeah. I guess." He's embarrassed by her compliment. "You should see the rest of the Dauphines. All sandy-haired, blue-eyed, golden gods and goddesses. It was quite the scandal when Grandpa came back from the war with a Japanese wife."

"I can see that. I wonder what it was like for her."

"Eventually everyone came to love her. She never spoke English though, but she sure as hell could understand it. You didn't want to be on the wrong end of her flip-flop if she caught you cursing, I tell you." He laughs at the memory of running down the hall of his childhood home while Granny chased him. "She was something else." He shakes his head. "Grandad called her his doll. I don't think he ever knew how racist he was. I wonder if she did." Henri gives a dry laugh and pulls a wooden chair from the other end of the porch to sit close. Bridgette pulls her feet up, tucking them under her skirt.

"There's room for two here," she says, her voice low, naturally sexy. Henri raises an eyebrow.

"Yeah?"

"Sure, it seems unfair to make you sit on that hard, wooden seat when there's so much room."

***

Bridgette feels his weight as he settles onto the lounge. With her eyes closed, she leans back against the cushions. The air is moist and smells of flowers and wet earth. She breathes deep and sighs. A breeze neither warm nor cool moves around them. "If I had a blanket, I could stay here forever," she says.

"Could you now?" Henri teases. She opens her lids and sees him watching again. His dark eyes intense. He's so close. She could sit up and be in his arms, or welcome him into hers.

"You mind if I stretch out?" she asks, straightening her legs. Her feet barely touch his thigh.

"Not at all." His eyes travel the length of her legs up past her knees to where her dress spreads around her. She shifts slightly, enough to make their contact intentional. Her toes rest on the smooth fabric against his legs.

"Your pants are really soft." She smiles and runs her toes up a few inches and back.

"Yeah?" His hand twitches beside her leg. His gaze stays on hers. Their desire, thicker than the humidity. Somewhere between the couch and the balcony she's given up fighting it. Henri is irresistible. Besides it's only the weekend, how far could she fall in three days?

"Yeah." She nods her head and giggles, still stroking his pant leg. "Why don't you stop being such a gentleman and touch me already?" His eyes widen and a half-grin crinkles the thin lines around them. In an instant, he's holding her feet in both hands. They are as warm and smooth as she had imagined. He strokes the tops of her feet, then his hands travel up slowly to her knee and back down. The sensation is as luxurious as the man himself. Her skin rejoices like a starving woman set before a banquet. Ripples travel up past her knee and beyond. She sits up, pulling her legs under her. His hands caress her knee, the outside of her thigh. Their faces, inches apart. His scent envelops her. "Do I have to tell you to kiss me too?" she asks. Then his lips are on hers, urgent, pressing. She kisses him back, her tongue playing at his lips, softening them, parting them slightly. His hand eases over her thigh and hip, around to her back to hold her close, leaving a trail of delicious sensations. Her nipples press against the fabric of her dress, aching to be against his bare chest. Their kisses grow deeper. He pulls away and she whimpers.

"You have to know this was not my intention," he says, his accent dripping with innocent charm.

"Who said it wasn't mine?" she tells him with a surety that surprises her. With her hands on his face, she pulls his face back to hers and straddles his lap. The hem of her skirt grazes her bare calves. His hands run up and down her back, and his lips trail over her chin and down her neck. With feather-light kisses, he follows the line of her collarbone. Her fingers work their way into his thick hair. She clutches it and tugs gently, tilting his face up to meet her lips again. Her tender parts are ablaze as she lowers herself onto his lap.

Panties, damp with expectation, press against the excitement behind his zipper. She sighs; a quiet moan escapes his throat. A horn from a passing car blares, and she jumps, startled, remembering herself and their surroundings. She'd forgotten about the traffic below, about the people walking by. She feels her cheeks redden and laughs at herself. "Sorry," she says as she slides off his lap, straightening her dress. Her heart is racing with an odd combination of excitement and dread. Her thoughts are everywhere all at once. Her mouth is suddenly dry, her throat tight. His nearness is too much. She feels an overwhelming desire to run.

"No apologies," Henri responds with a shake of his head, his discomfort apparent. "You can blame it on the reefer." He winks, laying one hand on her knee. She shifts out of his reach as subtly as she can.

"What time is it?" she asks, running her hand through her hair, to pull it off her shoulders, letting it fall on her back. She can't believe she's broken the barrier she set. *This can't happen. It's foolish.*

"It's about four o'clock," he says glancing at his watch.

"Well, shit," she responds, standing quickly. "I should get back to the Quarter. I've got a lot of work to do before tonight, and I bet Bunny is worried sick."

Chapter 6

"I almost fucked him," Bridgette tells her friend, with a lump of uncertainty lodged in her throat. Standing in the bathroom of her new hotel room, she's pulling her hair into a messy bun. It's smaller than the suite she shared with Bunny, but no less comfortable.

"Say what?" Bunny asks, leaning in the doorway. "Tell me everything."

Bridgette runs the water and lathers face wash in her palms. "He was actually kind of awful for a minute," she says before rubbing the sweet-scented foam on her face. Then after rinsing, she grabs a plush towel and pats dry. "Brunch was almost painful. The conversation was awkward to say the best. He reminded me of shit my dad used to say."

"That sucks. What turned it around?"

"Well, I'm not sure. He started showing me the city in a way I'd never seen it. I got to see the real him. Then we went to his place and he has the cutest dog."

"Wait a minute. You went to his house?"

"Yeah. Where the hell else do you think I almost fucked him?"

"He lured you there with a puppy?" Bunny raises one eyebrow and stares into the mirror, looking back at Bridgette.

"No. I wanted to see the Garden District, and he told me he has a house there. I asked him to take me there. He was a perfect gentleman. I made the first move," Bridgette snaps.

"But still, what if he hadn't been?"

"Oh, come on." Bridgette rolls her eyes and drops the towel on the sink. "I knew what I was doing."

"I'm sure that's what a lot of women think before they're raped and murdered in an alley somewhere." Bridgette sighs heavily and passes through the doorway. Bunny follows. "I'm serious, Bridgette."

"I know. And you're right. But I did know what I was doing and he was a perfect gentleman. I'm a pretty good judge of character. We spent hours together in public before *I* asked to see his place." Bridgette pulls her costume pieces out of her bag and lays them on the bed. Her anxiety rises again, whispering of constant doubt, questioning her every action. Bunny leans her hip against the wooden desk. "There was no luring. I invited myself to his place. The dog was a pleasant surprise."

"Sorry," Bunny says. "I wasn't insinuating that you couldn't take care of yourself. I started to worry after a few hours. Then Mike was lecturing me for letting you go alone. You weren't answering my texts, so my imagination got the better of me."

"Yeah. I'm sorry for not responding. I was…preoccupied," Bridgette says with a smile, pushing her discomfort deep down. "Now, are you done playing mama bear so I can tell you all the details?"

"Sure. But Mike's gonna have some papa bear words for you later, I'm sure."

"I expect nothing less from him. Where is he, anyway?"

"He's sleeping." Bunny's eyes light up and a small grin plays at the corners of her mouth. "Flying wears him out."

"I'm sure it was the flight." Bridgette rolls her eyes again. "Do you want to hear about my date or not?" she asks, unfurling the long white silk fans, watching them flutter in the mirror.

"Tell me everything," Bunny says as she pulls herself up onto the desk, sitting with legs crossed.

"Okay, so it started off well enough. The restaurant was beautiful and he looked amazing. It was picture perfect. But then he started talking. Or bragging, rather. It was an instant turnoff. Once we got past that, he shared some stuff about his family, which turned out to be depressing. So, I tried to steer the conversation to Trixie and how he knew her, but he was weird about that too. Wouldn't tell me where he disappeared to in high school or why."

"What do you think it is?" Bunny asks, leaning forward.

"I'm not sure, but he didn't want to talk about it."

"This isn't a strong case for going back to his place."

"Well, it got better. After we walked around for a while, I think he got comfortable and stopped trying to impress me. You know?"

"Yeah. I get it."

"So, after walking all over the Quarter, we went on a streetcar. He shared he had a place in the Garden District. Which happens to be my favorite part of New Orleans. As I've said, I insisted that he show me."

"That sounds about right."

"His house is beautiful, of course. Then he has this funny little mutt named Bones. A stray that he adopted."

"That's one way to your heart, for sure."

"It is. That and some good-ass weed."

"Ah, I see where this is going."

"Exactly. Once I saw how he was with his doggo, I could forgive the awkward conversation. I mean, some people aren't that good at small talk. Then we got stoned and hung out for a while. He has a sweet setup on his upper balcony, super cozy. One thing led to another…" Bridgette smiles, remembering his touch, his lips against hers. "I kind of attacked him."

"Of course you did." Bunny laughs and shakes her head. "So, how was it?"

"He was shy at first. Stopped me even. But once he assured me that it hadn't been his intention…"

"He did that?"

"Yeah, he did."

"Hm." Bunny looked thoughtful. "So, what happened then? Why'd you stop?"

"Well, we were out on his balcony and someone honked. The magic was lost. Then, I started questioning myself and realized what time it was and you know…here I am." Bridgette shrugs.

"You think he's coming tonight?"

"He said he wouldn't miss it. It's so strange. One minute I want nothing more than to be in his arms and the next… I don't know how to explain it. It's such a weird feeling." As she talks she struggles against the torrent of emotions in her chest.

***

Henri stands outside the Backdoor, which isn't a glamorous place. His watch reads close to ten o'clock. A poster on the door promises metal, mayhem, and mischief. Two bands' logos hover behind an image of Bridgette's friend Lilian. Her long black wig is combed gracefully over one pale shoulder. The full black ball gown highlights her curves. With dainty hands in opera gloves, she's holding the hem off the ground like a princess, revealing fishnet stockings and combat boots. One boot rests on top of a black skull. Henri snorts at the image. "Jesus," he mumbles under his breath, shaking his head.

The door swings open as he reaches for the handle. A large bearded man pushes through with his phone to his ear. "Excuse me," he says, brushing past Henri and walking out of earshot. Henri reaches for the door again as Bunny pushes through. She's looking radiant though concerned.

"Sorry, I didn't know anyone was there," she says. "It's you." She giggles, her gaze following the man.

"No worries. I'm the one lurking. I haven't missed the show, have I?"

"Nope. The first band's still on. They got started late. So, it will be a minute before their set is up. The girls are backstage getting ready. It's me and that one," she says with a grin, nodding at the guy who just passed him.

"You're not performing?" he asks, leaning against the wall. There's no reason to hurry in to see a band he has no desire to see.

"Nope. I'm here for moral support, and to keep Bridgette from wandering off with strangers." She pauses and looks down the alley at the man pacing on his phone. He gives a quick nod toward her and stands with his arms crossed over his chest still talking. "Let's hope I'm better at moral support."

"I'm sure you are. Besides, she didn't wander off, and I don't believe I'm a stranger anymore."

"I suppose not." She smiles a knowing smile and leans beside him. "Bridgette says you're a musician. What do you play?"

"A little bit of everything. But mostly guitar."

"Are you in a band?"

"I have been."

"Hmm," she hums, her eyes squinting with playful distrust. "Man of mystery, I see."

"Not at all. I'm not that interesting." He chuckles.

"We'll see about that." Her imposing date strides toward them with a look of concern. "Is everything all right?" she asks as he approaches. Henri is not a short man. But this guy makes him glad he's not interested in Bunny.

"Yeah. It was Vic," he says, shaking his head. "He had a question about his car. Must be a having a slow night. Everything's fine." He pulls Bunny into one large arm and levels his gaze on Henri.

"Henri." He introduces himself, extending his hand. "I met Miss Bunny last night with Bridgette."

"Mike." The guy responds with a grip that seems excessive.

"Next round's on me," Henri says, pulling the door open and holding it for them to enter the building.

"Sounds good to me," Mike answers as Bunny heads in before him. Henri follows behind, relieved that the first band's set is over.

***

"Trixie's up next. Then it's me," Bridgette says close to Bunny's ear over the sound of the crowd cheering for Charley's second routine. They are standing off stage to the right in an alcove for performers.

"These ladies are hardcore," Bunny states, clapping and cheering.

"Yeah, they are. Wait 'til you see Trixie though. You're going to love it."

"Up next," Lilian speaks into the microphone wearing a black silk robe hanging open over her bra and panties. "Back again, because we can't get enough of you guys…" The crowd cheers. Mike whistles from the bar. "Trixie Von Stamp."

Over the speakers, a child's voice sings "I'm a Little Teapot." Trixie lumbers through the crowd toward the stage, her oversize teapot costume bumping a couple of guys out of her way. "She couldn't fit her costume backstage." Bridgette laughs. Trixie makes it up the three steps with surprising ease. Bridgette cheers as Trixie struts back and forth across the stage, smiling and flirting. The teapot is one of the most impressive costumes she's ever seen, complete with a little lid as a hat. Trixie works the stage with comedy and grace. The audience is eating it up. Bridgette looks across the room at Henri. He's leaning against the bar, chatting with Mike, watching the show. The child's voice repeats the line like a broken record.

"When I get all steamed up… When I get all steamed up… When I get all steamed…" Then Ella Fitzgerald's rendition of "Steam Heat" begins to play. Trixie lifts the teapot over her head, revealing a sparkling corset and tutu in the same pink and blue of the teapot. The crowd erupts with applause. She shimmies and shakes through the song, dropping first the tutu, then the corset. As she bounces her ample breasts, steam emits from her pasties. It's amazing. Bridgette cheers and whistles, clapping her hands.

"That's something else," Bunny shouts over the cheers. "Are you ready?"

"I better be," Bridgette says, straightening the flowing white panels of her skirt. "I hate to follow that though." She laughs. Trixie comes bounding off stage. "That was amazing, Trixie."

"Thanks," she answers, out of breath.

She stands in the wings waiting for her cue. An absolute calm comes over her. She's always amazed at how easily she takes the stage. No nerves, no worries. Only the joy of movement, of connection to the music more than the audience. This is for her.

On stage, under the lights, surrounded by sound, she feels a oneness that can't be defined.

***

"Up next, we have a special surprise. Baby La Loop is here all the way from Chicago," Lilian announces with bravado. Henri claps and hoots. Mike, beside him, whistles and cheers. "Breezeblocks" by Alt-J plays loud over the speakers. Bridgette spins across the stage, a vision of perfection, dressed all in white and sparkling as the stage lights hit every rhinestone. Her long silken hair is piled in curls on top of her head. Her eyes and cheeks sparkle. Her smile beams. She bends, arches, and twirls, removing layer after layer of sheer white fabric. The audience responds with appreciative shouts and cheers.

Henri is hypnotized. *She moves like the wind* he thinks as she continues to dance. Now in her glittering bra and panties, she bends over for something and comes up with long white silk fans billowing around her. She twirls again, her dainty feet stepping and pointing. The curve of her hips, her shapely ass, her smooth, creamy stomach. Henri remembers the way she felt in his arms earlier that day. The way her lips had tasted. She holds the fans fluttering over her chest with one hand. With the other, she unlatches her bra. It hits the floor behind her. She's spinning again. The silk fans allowing momentary glimpses of her perky breasts. She opens her arms wide, revealing tiny pasties with tassels. They twirl as she bounces. The song fades out as the crowd cheers on. Her smile brightens as she spots him, blows a kiss, and runs off stage.

Chapter 7

Bridgette stands at the bar waiting for her water, her heart still racing. She wears a sheer vintage robe with fringe. "You are truly an artist," Henri says from beside her. His presence has an effect on her she'd rather not acknowledge. She remembers his lips on hers, the way his body felt against her.

"Thanks," she says, catching her breath. "What did you think of your first show?"

"It was entertaining. I imagine in another venue it would be even better."

"What, you don't like the Backdoor?" Bridgette asks, looking around the dank, dark club. With its low stage and giant speakers, it's set up for bands, not dancers.

"Oh, I like it for what it's intended. I was only saying that in a classier venue, one could make an evening out of it."

"Yeah, you're right. A good venue makes all the difference. It's much nicer when people are seated. Not standing so close, leering. My first time on stage was terrible."

"Was it? How?" he asks, line forms between his brows.

"Well, we double-booked for Halloween at a place we'd never been. It was directly after another show. We didn't have enough time to get from one place to the next. Not a good thing since Halloween shows always have a lot of costume and makeup. Which meant anyone performing in the first show couldn't really do the next. I'd been really wanting to do a solo routine. I'd been hooping mostly and backup dancing for other people up to that point. Everyone thought it would be a good way to get my feet wet. They were wrong." She laughs and drinks the cool water. Henri listens, smiling and sipping his drink. "It was awful. By the time we got there, the crowd was wasted. Like, lost their sense of personal boundaries and decency wasted. I went second. The audience was so close. Some guy tried to grab me."

"Really?" Henri asked, appalled.

"Yeah, really. Do you remember that, Bunny?" she asks, turning to see her snuggled into Mike's chest.

"Yeah. I remember Jonathan almost pulled you off stage and ended the show. He was so pissed."

"Was he?" Bridgette asked, surprised. "I don't remember that."

"Well, you were on stage, I was right beside him. He had words for Cin and Lucy later that night," Bunny shares.

"Did he really?" Bridgette asks, her cheeks warming with appreciation. "I didn't realize…" She thinks back to her early days with Burlesque A la Mode, how enamored she had been with it all. The dancers were so confident and talented. Jonathan was such a free spirit. She had fallen in love with them all. Jonathan in particular held a special place in her heart.

"But then you slapped that guy's hand away without missing a beat. It was awesome." Bunny laughs. "We knew you were one of us that night for sure."

"Trial by fire," Henri states.

"Something like that." Bunny laughs again.

"Wait a minute," Mike says to Bunny. "You said your first experience was terrible too." He quirks his brow. "I don't get it. If it's so shitty from the start, why would you keep doing it?" His serious blue eyes look from Bunny to Bridgette, then he shakes his head at Henri. Bridgette smiles at her best friend's levelheaded mate. The way his hand rests on Bunny's shoulder, his thumb brushing it absently. The way she looks up at him with hearts in her eyes. Bridgette wonders if that sort of love is possible for everyone. Or if they're some fluke of nature. Bridgette looks at Henri, who is watching her with rapt attention. Then she looks back at Mike.

"Until you've done it, you will never understand," Bridgette responds.

"Oh, he'll never do it." Bunny laughs. "Believe me, I've tried. He takes himself too seriously."

"Yep," Mike says, resolute.

"How about you, Henri?" Bunny asks. Bridgette turns to him with a smile. He's grinning back, shaking his head.

"I'll leave it to you ladies. You're far better than I could ever hope to be," he says, putting on his Southern charm. He tilts his head in a way that, despite his height, makes him appear to be looking up.

It reminds her of their afternoon's embrace, of how it felt to be so close to him. She leans in close, tempted to steal a kiss.

"You might surprise yourself," she teases. "I bet you've got some moves."

"Moves, I have. I'm more selective of who I share them with."

"Excuse me?" Bridgette snaps and pulls away, thinking of the judgment she'd received from her grandparents and father since she started performing. New Orleans was the last place she thought she would hear it. "Maybe I should be too." She rolls her eyes, turning to the bartender to refill her water.

"Bridgette. I meant no offense," he stammers. "I only meant that I don't believe anyone wants to see me dancing." He gestures to the people milling around the stage, waiting for the next band. "These folks surely don't."

"No, I don't imagine they do," Bridgette states, turning her attention to Bunny and Mike. Her cheeks burn with irritation as she shakes her head.

"Please, *cher,*" he pleads. "I chose my words poorly. I only meant that I don't have the guts or the glamour to entertain anyone the way you did." He raises both eyebrows and smiles an awkward smile. "Let me make it up to you. Buy you a drink? Are you hungry?"

Her stomach growls on cue. "I am, actually."

"May I buy you a late dinner?" he asks, smiling. Bridgette looks him over. She's still irritated, but willing to give him another chance. Plus, food is the best way to her heart.

"I could eat," she responds, with a glance toward Bunny and Mike. They're standing close, talking in low voices, holding hands. "You guys hungry?"

Bunny looks over her shoulder with a shrug. "Meh." She turns back to Mike. He's watching her with a smile. He raises an eyebrow. "I mean, I guess I'm a little hungry."

"If you can untangle yourself from your man, I could use some help with my stuff backstage." Bridgette pokes.

"Ha. Ha. Funny," Bunny responds, laughing as she pulls one leg from between Mike's and releases his hands.

"We'll be right back," Bridgette says to Henri. "Don't let this guy scare you." She motions to Mike.

"You're scarier than me, Bridgette," Mike says, finishing his beer in one swallow.

"I'll take that as a compliment," she replies with a lift of her chin. Spotting Lilian and Charley heading backstage, she and Bunny hurry to meet them.

***

"So, where do we go from here?" Bridgette, asks sitting beside him, her phone in hand. Bunny and Mike sit opposite. Empty plates fill the table before them. "I don't think Lilian, Charley, and Trixie are going to join us like they said." Henri's relieved at the thought. Trixie's presence made his past an inevitable conversation topic. Given enough time and thought, she would eventually remember the circumstances of his disappearance. It'd been all over the news. Though his parents' money could do a lot of things, it couldn't affect people's memories. Trixie would eventually remember. All he could hope was that it would be well after Bridgette had left town. The thought of her leaving before they had a chance to get to know each other bothers him as much as her finding out about his past. Though she makes him feel whole, he knows it's fleeting and she'll be gone too soon. Leaving him like the streets after Mardi Gras, one big empty mess.

"Wanna check out the Carousel Bar back at the hotel?" Bunny asks from across the table. She's leaning against Mike, her head on his shoulder. Henri admires the couple. Bunny is soft and lovely with a gentle voice that carries laughter in every word while Mike, with his large build and scholarly wit, has a more serious demeanor. Their depiction of the masculine and feminine archetypes would be comical if it weren't so natural. They seem addicted to the other's touch, and Henri looks to Bridgette beside him and understands. He's unnervingly aware of the absence of hers. Their day together hadn't been perfect, but the good parts had been better than any he could have imagined. It had been heaven to touch her, to hold her in his arms, yet knowing she'd be leaving in a day makes the fleeting intimacy painful.

"I'm down," Bridgette responds, dropping her napkin on her plate. She'd traded in her flowing white and glittering costume for an oversize t-shirt and shorts. With her face cleaned of elaborate makeup, her curled and pinned hair is the only remnant of her time on stage. As tantalizing as she was while performing, she's more stunning now.

"Shall we?" Henri slides from the booth and stands, offering his hand to Bridgette. She takes it, but only to lift herself from her seat. She quickly turns and reaches to retrieve her bag from beneath the booth. As she bends, her shorts reveal more of her tanned and tattooed thighs. The oversize t-shirt slides up to show her back. Though she'd been almost naked on stage, this display is irresistible. Bunny notes his leering with a giggle as she passes by. He looks away quickly. Mike offers an understanding chuckle and holds fast to Bunny's hip. "Here, let me," Henri offers Bridgette as she stands with her bag.

"I've got it," she says, slinging the bag over her shoulder. "My costume's pretty light." She laughs and heads for the door. Henri watches as her hidden curves sway under her shirt.

***

"This place has quite the gimmick," Henri says as the carousel bar begins its second turn since their arrival. The mirrors, lights, and carved smiling cherubs shine down on the foursome. Bridgette and Bunny are giggling, two Sazeracs in and ordering their third.

"That it does," Mike says from beside Bunny, nursing his only beer. His hand rests on her knee. "I don't know how you two are drinking that poison."

"It's easy." Bunny bats her lashes and downs the last of her drink with a large swallow and a wince. Bridgette cackles and does the same.

"Now I want to do shots," Bridgette exclaims with wide eyes, waving at the bartender.

"Perfect," Bunny agrees.

Henri sees his limited time with Bridgette disappearing quickly with every drink she has. He can't imagine that she'd take kindly to his suggesting that she take it easy, though. The bartender returns with their mixed drinks, looking irritated.

"We'll settle up," Mike says before they can order a round of shots.

"Oh, come on, Mike," Bunny snaps.

"Really, Amanda? You want a hangover tomorrow? 'Cause this is how you get a hangover tomorrow."

Henri watches and waits, thankful for Mike's interjection, and is curious how it will play out. Bunny squints her eyes and scrunches her face for a long, silent pause.

"You're not my daddy. Stop acting like it," she says, sipping her fresh drink with a surly pout. Henri sits, surprised by the shift from her usual sunny demeanor.

"Come on, Amanda. You don't think you've had enough?" Mike asks calmly.

"No, Mike. I don't think I've had enough." She glares at him with malice that shocks Henri. The two stare at each other for what feels like an eternity. Bridgette sips her drink and scrolls through her phone, seemingly unaware of the tension building between her friends. Mike presses his lips together into a tight line. He runs a hand through his beard and sighs, glancing at Henri.

"You are going to be sick as a dog tomorrow if you finish *this* one. And now you want to start doing shots?"

"Jesus Christ. What am I, a fucking toddler?" Bunny lifts her drink to her lips and takes a long pull from the straw.

"From the looks of it? Yes." The irritation in Mike's voice has Henri on edge. He looks to Bridgette again. She looks up from her phone and shakes her head with an odd little smile.

Bunny turns in her seat, her back to Henri. He stands awkwardly, trying not to watch the exchange. Mike frowns and blinks slowly then pushes his beer away. "I know, if it were me, I'd like to be in top shape for tomorrow," he says quietly, while his fingers run along the side of her knee. Henri sips his drink and looks up, waiting for Bunny to explode.

"Ugh. I don't even want this now," Bunny whines, pushing her drink away. "You two okay if we turn in?" She looks at Bridgette with her signature giggle, her face beaming again.

"I think we'll be all right," Bridgette says with a half-smile.

"You sure?" Bunny lowers her voice as though Henri can't hear her.

"Yeah, I'm sure." Bridgette looks to Mike. "Will you get her out of here already?"

"Gladly." Mike laughs and stands to leave, takes Bunny's hand and guides her down from the slowly rotating bar seat.

"Oh shit." She giggles as she steps down, almost toppling into Mike's arms. "Good night," she says, the booze thick in her words. "Love you." She leans into Bridgette with a heavy hug.

"Good to meet you, Henri," Mike says with a polite smile and a look in his eyes that borders on intimidation. "'Night, Bridgette." His smile warms. "Be safe."

"Bye, Henri," Bunny calls with a poor attempt at his accent and a smile that makes it forgivable.

"Those two are something else," Bridgette says, sipping her drink. She turns to Henri, shaking her head.

"Yeah. What was that all about?" Henri asks, running his fingers through his hair.

"What was what?" Bridgette raises an eyebrow. "Bunny can't handle her liquor." She chuckles and waves her hand in dismissal. Henri looks at her curiously. "That's nothing. You should see what happens if he doesn't stop her."

"Really?" Henri asks, still dumbfounded. He doesn't understand real relationships. They confuse him. He's never had one, and his family didn't exactly provide an example he could follow. He could've sworn Mike and Bunny were going to have a knockdown drag-out, and then poof, a few meaningful glances, some affection, and they're fine.

"Really." Bridgette nods again and tucks her phone away in her bag. "Don't worry about them." She says taking a sip from her drink. Their eyes meet over the glass. Time seems to stop and Bridgette places her drink on the bar, pushing it away. A message he doesn't miss.

"When are you flying out?" he asks, pushing his empty glass away.

"Monday morning." Her gaze drops to her hands in her lap. She looks back at him with sparkling eyes.

"Well, that means we've got a lot to see tomorrow, don't we." He smiles at her. His heart thumps an irregular beat in his chest. It's an aching sort of discomfort that he's not familiar with. He's no stranger to beautiful women, and no stranger to desire. But there's something more happening with Bridgette. Something he understands but doesn't want to feel. The air seems lighter when she's near. Henri knows he could get used to it despite the fact that she'll be gone before he can.

"I guess we do," she says, her voice soft and low. She blinks and holds his gaze with hers, communicating loud and clear without saying a word. "Where do we start?"

Chapter 8

In a flurry of excitement, Bridgette pulls Henri by the hand into the empty elevator, pushes the button for her floor, and the doors slide shut. He's behind her, leaning against the handrail, looking delectable in the same pants he had on that morning. The fabric of his black shirt is silky and lightweight. It begs to be touched, stroked. She remembers how she had wanted to undo his buttons that morning and feels the heat rise to her face at the thought of actually doing it. She takes in his long, toned arms as they rest on the rail on either side of him. His wristwatch shines under the muted light from above. He grins with a glint in his eye. A lush sort of anxiety hangs on their unspoken words.

"I really had a great time with you today," she says softly, stepping toward him.

"That's music to my ears, *cherie.*"

"Is it?" She steps closer.

"It is. Seems the only thing I've wanted to do since I met you is to please you."

"Oh?" She's now inches away from his toned body, close enough to smell his intoxicating scent. She inhales deeply and bats her lashes. "Then do it," she goads.

Lust burns in his eyes, and his grin disappears. He raises one hand to her cheek. While his thumb strokes her face, his fingers play at the back of her ear and neck. The sensation dances down her spine. Her nipples brush against the fabric of her baggy t-shirt. Painfully slow, his lips come down on hers, so soft. His other hand rests on her cheek while he's barely grazing her mouth with his. She whimpers into the kiss, longing for more. But he continues with his delicate exploration. Her tongue darts and flicks, urging him on. His fingers move down her neck to her shoulders, thumbs stroking her collarbone. The elevator stops with a slight lurch. Her eyes flutter open. His are staring down with intensity.

"This is my floor," she whispers. Henri's hands fall away as he stands, swiping his hair out of his eye. The air is cold with the absence of his touch, and she smiles a shy smile as she leads him out of the elevator and down the hall.

At her door she turns to see him following close behind. His hands in his pockets, he's strolling along, cool and collected. *How many times has he done this?* she wonders. "I've never done anything like this," she says, scanning her key card. With the buzz and a click, she pushes the door open. An icy blast from the air conditioner greets them.

"What do you mean?"

"I don't go around luring men back to my hotel rooms."

"I don't imagine you do," he says, following her in. She closes the door behind him and flips on every light she passes. What she felt in the elevator is fading. She's questioning her decision as she crosses the room to switch off the air conditioner.

"It's just…" Feeling foolish, she turns to see him standing, his shoulder leaned against the wall, a playful smile on his lips. Those heavenly lips that felt so perfect against hers. "I don't know what I'm doing." A small laugh escapes her chest. "I see you and I want you. Then I'm near you and I want you even more." She sighs. "But I barely know you." The king-size bed dominates the room between them. It screams its silent demand to be shared with someone. "Yet, I don't care." He's watching her patiently. His gaze never leaving her face. The crinkles around his eyes match his perfect smile.

"Would you like me to leave?"

"No. That's the problem. I know that I should, but it's the last thing in the world I want."

"How about I go and get some ice," he says, reaching for the ice bucket. "I imagine you'll appreciate a cool drink after putting away those Sazeracs. You get comfortable. If you like me to leave when I get back, no worries. I'll be here first thing in the morning to take you for breakfast."

"Okay," she agrees with a heavy sigh. She's moved by his concern for her comfort. His willingness to walk away from what he must've surely thought was a done deal. Why wouldn't she want to share a night with a handsome man in a beautiful suite in an enchanting city? Sure, back home she would make him wait. They would date for weeks before she shared her bed with him. But she wasn't back home. She didn't have weeks. She'd be gone in two days. Maybe it would be better if she made him leave and lost his number.

What is it about him? How had he slid so smoothly past all her defenses? She slumps onto the bed and starts pulling at the pins in her hair. As each curl falls, she relaxes more, caring less about the things she should or would do, and more about what she can do. Shaking her hair out, she scratches her scalp and fluffs it.

There's a gentle knock at the door.

She hurries to answer it.

***

Full ice bucket in hand, Henri heads back to the room, not surprised Bridgette is nervous. In a way, he is too. With her soft skin and pouted lips he'd barely had time to fully enjoy, the woman is an irresistible temptation. On stage, she's glittering and full of life, spinning directly into his heart, a heart primed by her earlier that day on his balcony when she took charge. Her actions stating clearly what she wanted. Then in the elevator, so forward. He stands at the door, his heart in his throat. *Please don't send me home.*

The door swings open. She's standing in that same oversize t-shirt. Her hair is down, a cloud of fluffy curls around her shoulders, and a full beaming smile on her face. "I want you to stay," she says, pulling him forward by his shirt.

She closes the door and locks it behind him. He barely has time to set the ice bucket aside before she's on him, tugging at the buttons of his shirt. Her hands working one after another until it hangs open, revealing his bare chest and stomach. He's thankful for his gym membership as she slides her hands down the length of his torso. Then she's holding his face in her hands, pressing her lips to his without restraint. She bites at his bottom lip and leads him by his open shirt away from the door, stepping back heading them toward the bed. As she bumps it, she looks up with a start. A wicked smile spreads across her face as she eases up one knee then the other.

With her gaze on his, she slips the t-shirt over her head, shaking her hair out. It spills over her shoulders. She's completely nude and it's nothing like what he saw on stage.

She's raw and perfect for him alone. Her dainty pink nipples stand pointed, demanding attention. Henri dips his head to taste one, sucking it into his mouth, his tongue tracing the thin red line left by her pasties. She sighs and runs her fingers through his hair. He's feasting, moving back and forth from one delicious nipple to the other, delirious from the taste and scent of her.

His cock aches against his pants. Her hands travel down his torso to find him, stroking his rock-hard dick though the fabric. He lets out a low growl, and she answers by tugging at his belt, then working the button and zipper open to release him.

Her hands are soft and warm, running the length of his shaft. He shivers with pure elation, reveling in the feel of what she's doing, and that it's her doing it. She strokes and squeezes until he seeks her mouth again, diving in, taking everything he can from the wet warmth while dueling with her tongue. Her hands travel his torso again, sliding up his chest to his shoulders, pulling his shirt down his arms. She presses her breasts to his chest.

Henri is consumed by her.

His name is a sigh on her breath, and his pulse quickens at the sound. Sliding his hand down her back, he lowers her to the bed. His lips travel from her mouth down her neck, sucking at her delectable breasts again. He grazes his cheek down her stomach, tongue darting around her navel.

Her skin tastes salty and sweet. He settles on his knees and kisses her hip bones, her smooth mound, breathing in her female scent. He dips his tongue to taste her and finds a tangy nectar he could become addicted to. She's squirming. Goosebumps spring up over her flesh as she begins to writhe.

Holding her hips in his hands, he tastes her again, rolling his tongue over her swollen clit. She twitches and squeals, her back arching to him. He spreads her knees apart, exploring every fold of her lush lower lips, lapping up her earthy nectar. She's moaning, one hand in his hair, the other gripping the duvet cover. His hands stroking the soft skin of her inner thigh while his tongue explores her most sensitive places, lapping her juices, teasing her clit.

His cock is throbbing nearly to the point of pain, but he can't stop tasting her. He runs his knuckles down her thighs, then opens her sex, spreading it wide with his fingers. His thumbs dance over her opening. His tongue finds her swollen clit again. He toys with it while she writhes. He sucks at it gently and slides his thumb into her warm, wet slit. She sighs as he plays a slow rhythm on her body. Then she coos and rocks with him. He picks up the tempo until she's grinding down on his face and thumb with her frenzied chase, and then she cries out, pulling his hair by the roots, her hot channel convulsing around his thumb.

He pulls her clit into his mouth, and slides his thumb out slowly then dips his tongue to lap at her sweet juices. She pants and lets go of his hair, trying to close her legs. He holds fast, wanting to devour her. She twists herself and pulls away, laughing. Henri looks down at her beautiful bare body, splayed on the bed. Her bright eyes peek out from the mass of tousled hair and he knows as delicious as this has been, it's about to get better.

***

Bridgette looks up at Henri, who is above her, his pants open, cock standing erect. His expression is full of a wild hunger. He runs his tongue over his shining white teeth in an animal display. She's a puddle and he's only begun to give her the pleasure she knows he's capable of.

Brushing her hair away from her face, she sits up, pulling her feet over to make room for him. He kicks out of his shoes, drops his pants to the floor, and lowers himself onto the bed beside her. His hands are everywhere at once, her skin alight with sensation. Every nerve ending seems frayed while clamoring for contact. Sated and somehow still starving.

He's warm and smooth under her hands as she explores his toned and flawless skin. A tattoo of cherry blossoms creeps down one shoulder, spreading out over his back around his ribs on the opposite side. He's at her breasts again, kissing and suckling. Ripples of the best kind of torment cascade over her. Her hands reach for his shaft, silken steel and blazing. She quivers at the thought of taking him inside of her.

Pushing him back onto the bed, she straddles him. His rigid heat prods at her clit, still alight from his expert attention. She glides down, met with utter bliss as he fills her completely. His gaze flashes as it meets hers. She runs her hands over his chest, reveling in the luxurious feel of him. He grabs her hips as he thrusts slow and deep, grinding into her. She shudders from her toes through to the roots of her hair, feeling another orgasmic wave.

Rocking with his thrusts, she grips at his chest, teeth clenched, moaning and whimpering. Her release pours like a flood over her and she collapses to his chest. He strokes her back and kisses her face through the mass of tangled hair. Her heart pounds, breath heaving.

Gently, he lays her on her back, brushing her hair away from her face. She's lost somewhere between heaven and the pillow. He kisses her face again, her open mouth, first her top lip then the bottom. So delicately it almost hurts. Then, he's above her, entering slowly, hips rolling with the tempo of her heavy breath. She sighs and crumbles under the strokes. Her eyes fall on the cherry blossoms on his shoulder. So clear and rich with detail, down to every pistil and stamen, every tiny bud and crackling branch. The varied shades of pink are beautiful against his skin.

Pleasure like she's never known runs the length of her body as he fills her again and again with his skilled and tender strokes. She's there again in that place of rapturous awe that he's already taken her twice. It's slower this time, like a tide rising over her, surrounding her until she's lost in delirium. Then, he's moving faster, stroking harder, his release a slow groan when he buries his face in her neck.

After his breathing evens out, he rises on one elbow and on his perfect face is a contented grin and sparkling eyes.

***

Bridgette wakes with a start. Every light in the room is on. Henri is lying on his stomach beside her. She takes in his sleeping form. The tattoo across his back is breathtaking with the same intricate cherry blossoms as on his shoulder. They cascade over magnolias done in fine detail, covering most of his back. A strand of pearls hangs from a branch, almost hidden among all the lovely pink flowers. She may have missed it if it hadn't been done with such skill. They seem as luminous as the real thing, almost catching light.

She looks down at the pearls on her thigh and laughs. She had once thought her tattoo artist was the best. Seeing Henri's back in full light proved otherwise. *How many hours had it taken?* she wonders, then remembers the bucket of ice.

Cool water and a hot shower beckon her from across the room.

Chapter 9

Henri wakes before Bridgette. She's sprawled beside him deep in sleep, face buried in her pillow, one leg peeking out from beneath the blankets. He longs to stroke her bare skin, to taste her as he had the night before, but she's content in sleep and he has no idea how she'll respond to being woken with his mouth on her body. Would she roll into his arms, welcoming his touch, or would she recoil, disappointed in her lapse of judgment? He watches a moment longer. Her soft, heavy breathing assures him she'll be out for a while. *Best to give her space.* A good lie he tells himself as he slips off the bed and dresses quietly. He's a coward. Leaving because staying would mean he'd have more of Bridgette. More memories to plague him when she leaves.

He pens a note, places the pad on the bedside table, pulls the shades closed tight, and shuts off the lights, holding his shoes in his hand.

Sunday morning in the Quarter is as bustling as any day. There's a weight to the clouds that has people moving quicker than usual. The air, though heavy, is still. It pulls at his clothes, dampening his skin. His hair lies flat and lifeless. He rushes to the catch the next streetcar. It's half full, mostly locals. He takes a seat and watches out the window as he replays last night. She's everything he thought she would be and more. Soft and fierce, responsive and inquisitive, and she tastes like heaven. Tangy honey he can still taste on his lips, in his mouth, and down his throat. He grins, remembering her orgasms.

Had it been only yesterday they'd had their awkward ride to his place, and the innocent way her hand in his had made his stomach drop like an untried adolescent?

The streetcar stops, and a family of four take the seats across from him, dressed for church, or brunch, or both. A lovely mother, handsome father, a boy, and a girl. Both young and sweet, watching out the windows, pointing and exclaiming at everything they see.

The mother catches his gaze and smiles a proud smile, stroking her son's shiny gold hair. Henri nods with an easy smile and turns his attention back to the window.

Bridgette would make an excellent mother. Where the hell did that thought come from? Family had never been in his plans. He enjoys being Uncle Henri, who carries his nieces and nephews around on his back and plays silly games. He's the one to bring strange and extravagant gifts to infuriate his siblings. The louder the better is his general rule. The more assembly required, the more he likes it.

But seeing the family across from him, so sweet and lovely, with Bridgette ever-present in his mind, for the first time in all his life he feels a tiny pang of regret for the vasectomy he elected to have years before. It had been a brilliant idea at the time and surely saved him a multitude of disasters. Yet, on this slow and dreamy morning, inspired by new emotions, he wonders if he jumped the gun and made that decision before he found a woman who could stir his soul.

Don't be a fool, he tells himself and pushes the wayward thoughts away. *She'll be gone in a day and you'll be back to life as usual.* Until now, that's how he liked it. A few days of seduction, then good-bye. Enjoy your life. Thanks for the memories. Mostly, his liaisons are with out-of-towners, and occasionally he likes to dabble with the locals. One-night stands with girls having a good time with their friends. Bartenders, waitstaff, even that Uber driver recently. She'd been fun. Also, the reason he now used Lyft or the streetcars.

He feels empty thinking of Bridgette's imminent departure. It rattles him in time with the streetcar's journey down the street, shaking and stopping and starting again. Like him, knowing he wants something he can't and shouldn't have, but starting to think again of how his heart will feel after Bridgette is gone.

The beautiful family departs. He waits for his stop, his heart aching.

His street is quiet as he walks along the uneven sidewalk, each dip and crack familiar to him. The blooms in the gardens waft their heavenly scents across the still air. Henri breathes deep. There's something about the overcast days that makes the flowers smell sweeter. He wishes Bridgette were with him as he swings the gate open. Bones is there to meet him at the door. Henri kneels to scratch him around the neck. The old mutt sniffs and roots around his shirt, wagging his tale. "You can smell her, huh, boy? You liked her, didn't you?" Henri says softly with an empty laugh. "Me too." He stands aside to let Bones bounce happily into the yard, oblivious of the pain in Henri's chest.

Inside, it's dark and cool. He could climb the stairs and fall into bed. Push her out of his mind and try to forget he ever met her. But he doesn't see how when every time he closes his eyes she's there. He drops his clothes in a pile in the bathroom and turns on the shower. The water runs hot from the shower head, and he steps under it, soaking his hair. The finely scented suds run down his frame as he goes through the motions absently. It does nothing to revive him. He stands, numb, remembering the last time he'd felt so empty.

Sixteen years old and broken. His mother was riding beside him in the back of their long black Mercedes. She wouldn't look at him. Her face was turned toward the window, her hands in her lap. "Your father and I don't know what to do with you," she said quietly, twirling the ring on her index finger.

He fought his tears as she waited for a response. "I'm so sorry." He choked on the words, the tears spilling. What had started as an adventure had ended in tragedy. Empty didn't explain the feeling in his chest. A life gone, and it was his fault. There was nothing he could do about it.

"I know, baby, I know." Her voice warmed as she turned and pulled him into her arms. He sobbed freely into her silk shirt, tears soaking her shoulder.

"I don't want to go," he cried.

"I know. I know. I don't want you to go. But it's the only option we have right now." Her voice quavered. She held him so tight.

"I want to go to the funeral. I want to see her." His sobbing continued.

"You know you can't do that, Henri. The sooner you're away from here the better."

"But I didn't mean to. I didn't mean for anyone to get hurt."

"No, no you didn't. I know. We all know. But that doesn't make it better. That doesn't bring her back. And her parents..." He could feel her lose her battle with tears as her words trailed off. The emptiness grew in his chest as they cried together. The airport loomed closer as the wide, open finality of death was too great to comprehend. His young mind struggled to process that he had caused it.

"What about Dad?" he asked, clinging to his mother like the scared little boy he was.

She sighed heavily. "He'll take care of everything. He'll be okay." She released Henri from her embrace and straightened beside him. He slouched against the seat, numbness creeping over him. She broke the silence. "Your great-grandma is old, but she's sharp and capable. Her driver will pick you up. You'll be on your own over there. Please, I beg of you, stay out of trouble. We'll get you home as soon as possible." Her words fell on ears deafened by self-loathing and fear.

"Fuck." Henri sighs, letting the hot water run over his head. How long had it been since he thought of that day? His time in Japan ended up being wonderful, all his years abroad had. But they were born from such ugly circumstances, he had to compartmentalize it. That morning in the car with his mother followed the worst night of his life. A night best forgotten.

Unlike last night. Last night was a heaven he didn't deserve, but oh how he craves more.

***

Bridgette wakes slowly, running her legs over the fine fabric of the sheets. Henri's scent lingers beside her. She's sad to find him gone, but the note at her bedside, written in fine script, assures her he'll return with coffee. She sighs, remembering the slow and tender way he kissed and touched her. She's never been with a man so patient for his own pleasure. They always rushed to get their dicks wet. But Henri acted as if he would've waited all night. There's a tremor of arousal as she recalls little details of their love play, his fingertips on her skin, his smiling lips, the sparkle in his eyes as she rode him.

"Shit," she says, realizing her mistake. No wonder it felt so good. They didn't use a condom. "You, dumbass." She sits up to check her period calendar on her phone. *Damn it. I can't believe I'm so dumb.* The dates on her calendar are a comfort. She's days past her fertility window. What was she thinking? The last thing she needed was to get knocked up from a one-night stand. Seems she would have learned from her mother's mistakes. The mistake she talked about often. Never considering that the mistake she spoke of was Bridgette, and her mother had shown her she was a burden all her life. Left behind or taken along begrudgingly. Bridgette's existence the reason for all her mother's problems.

She was in the backseat of her mother's car, her backpack stuffed with her belongings. "Why can't we stay with Grandma and Grandpa?" she remembered asking as her mom pulled out of their driveway.

"Because they don't want us, baby," her mom had said, looking at her in the rearview mirror. She couldn't have been more than five years old. Though they proved they loved her dearly over the years, she never would forget the way her tiny heart broke upon hearing those words.

She shakes her head, refusing to let the memories ruin her morning. Turning her thoughts to Henri's smile instead.

God, I hope he's clean. Either way, it can't happen again. But how she wants it to happen again. She would be happy to spend the entire day on this bed as long as he's in it with her. She wonders how long he's been gone, and when he'll return.

Then she texts Bunny.

I did it. I fucked him.

Her phone chimes before she sets it down.

What?

How was it?

Bridgette smiles at the question, not sure how much she wants to share. Her fingers fly quickly with her response.

He was amazing. Like nothing I've ever had.

I'm not surprised. Where are you?

In my room. He went for coffee. I'll call you later.

Bridgette stands to dress, stretching her arms over her head. The room seems empty without him. Throwing on a long, loose sundress, she straightens the blankets on the bed and settles in to wait for Henri's return. With the accordion music he introduced her to playing, she relaxes against the pillows piled high and attempts to find him on social media. Her search is fruitless.

There's a light knock at the door. Her heart leaps and she springs to her feet to answer. He's there with a coffee in each hand and a silly grin. "Good morning," he says, his voice smooth as honey.

"Good morning." She smiles back, taking the coffee he offers, stepping aside to let him in. His leg brushes her dress. A shimmer of excitement slides up her spine at the brief contact.

"Sorry I left. It was early and I hadn't planned on staying out all night. Had to get home to check on Bones." Her cheeks warm with appreciation that he cares so much about his dog.

He went all the way across town to check on his puppy. "Did he manage okay without you?" she asks.

"He's all right. Spent many nights on his own before he met me, I'd wager. Now he gets to do it on designer furniture." He chuckles and leans against the desk.

"Of course, he does," Bridgette says. "How is it outside?"

"Hot," he says with a grimace, "and still. Feels like a storm is coming."

"So, what are we going to do today?" She sits on the bed, sipping her coffee. It's strong and dark, exactly the way she likes it.

"I had big plans," he says, watching her from across the room. "But seeing you now… Maybe I'd like to change them."

"What were your plans?" She bats her lashes. "This coffee is perfect, by the way."

He smiles. "Well, there's a little café not far from here with better beignets then Café Du Monde. Then, a few places that I think you'd enjoy. I was thinking dinner at Baccanal. They do a charcuterie spread to die for." He sits on the foot of the bed, taking her feet in his hands. "Or we could order room service and stay here all day."

"All of that sounds wonderful." She moans, reveling in his touch. "I wish we could do both."

"There is so much that I wish we could do," he says, his hands moving slowly up her leg, under her long skirt. His touch is thrilling. His voice decadently sexy.

"Wait." She stops his hand from creeping any farther. "We made a mistake last night." Henri pulls his hand away. The color drains from his face.

"I'm so sorry. I thought you were—"

"Oh no, I was, I was. Oh god I was," she says, smiling and nodding her head vigorously. "I was talking about protection." She sits up and takes his hand to her chest. "We can't do anything else until we've talked about it. Last night was reckless and so out of character."

"Oh, thank god." He sighs, his shoulders relaxing.

"I'm sorry it came out weird, but you were touching me and I was ready to do it all again. I blurted the first thing that came to mind."

"So, you're ready to do it all again?" He brings her hand to his lips with a grin.

"Mm-hmm." She nods, a gentle, rolling excitement building as his lips brush her knuckles.

"I'm clean. I get tested regularly," he says, holding her hand in both of his. Then he looks away with a curious sort of darkness. "Pregnancy isn't an issue."

"Oh?" She's unsure of the proper response.

"I had a vasectomy years ago. Seemed like the best idea at the time." He smiles and shrugs.

"I see." She looks at him, puzzled by the feeling of disappointment washing through her. "That's a relief."

"But if you're more comfortable with protection. I understand completely. There's a drugstore on every corner in this town." He smiles and kisses her knuckles again. "Your call."

"I think it'll be okay," she says, melting into him, leaning in for more. His lips are on hers, soft and longing. She's sighing happily, lost in the sensation. Then her stomach growls loud enough for him to hear. He pulls away abruptly with a chuckle.

"You're hungry."

"Oh my god," she mutters, embarrassed. "Yes."

"Come on." He stands and offers his hand with another chuckle. "Let's go get some food."

Chapter 10

The beignets are delicious, though Henri eats most of them. Bridgette's café au lait is the highlight of breakfast, the rich and creamy cup a delightful departure from her normal go to cuppa joe. Henri holds her hand as they stroll through the French Market. Vendors are everywhere, some sitting patiently, others shouting like carnival barkers trying to sell their wares. She carries a couple small bags, some trinkets she couldn't pass up. Mostly jewelry, and a set of beautifully painted fans she could surely use in a routine someday.

"I wish you'd let me buy those for you," Henri says as they walk away from her most recent purchase.

"Don't be silly. I might not be swimming in money like you, but I budgeted for this trip, and I want to treat myself."

"I know, but I want to spoil you." He stops and pulls her into his arms, looking down with a sweet smile.

"I appreciate it, really. I'll let you spoil me in other ways," she tells him, raising her brows with a sexy smirk.

"I'm looking forward to it." He kisses her with gentle passion. The clamor of people passing by disappears as the world becomes only Henri, his warm lips, and his embrace. His lips leave hers, startling her back to reality. "Now, let's keep moving. There's so much to see."

The stalls give way to shops with open walls. They part ways; Henri busies himself, trying on hats. Bridgette finds silk scarfs to admire. One in particular looks like watercolors painted in the deep blues and greens of the ocean with cream-colored fringe along both ends. It's simple, but beautiful and far too expensive. "What do you think?" Henri comes around the corner looking like a Cuban drug lord in his light-colored shirt and pants and a straw panama hat. Bridgette laughs despite how attractive he is.

"It really works on you," she says, nodding.

"Really? You think? I feel like my grandpa." He grins.

"You're a pretty sexy grandpa."

"Yeah? Maybe I'll get it. I never shop down here. It's kind of fun actually."

"It is." Her phone rings. "It's Bunny, I'm gonna take it out there," she says, angling her head at the bench outside. "Hey," she answers.

"Hey, how's your day going?"

"Great actually. We're in the French Market now. Going to check out some shops in the Quarter next. What're you doing?"

"Mike's been watching satellite maps all morning. He's worried about the weather. He thinks we might get stuck here."

"Really? It's that bad?"

"Not yet. But you know him, he's got to have a plan for everything. The idea of being stuck in an airport to wait out a storm is killing him."

"That sounds like him. So, what's his plan then?"

"He's talking about leaving tonight or postponing our flight until later in the week. He wanted me to hear your thoughts."

Bridgette's heart jumps at the idea of spending more time here with Henri. "I know which I'd prefer."

"I bet you do. How are things going with Henri?"

"I'm having a lot of fun and wishing we had more time together. I'd love to stay longer. But I don't want to be stuck in a hurricane."

"I don't think it's going to get that bad. At least I hope not."

"Well, shit. Let me talk to Henri and call you back. He's a local, maybe he knows what to expect." She hangs up.

He's coming out to the shop carrying a bag, wearing his new hat, looking amazing. "I feel like a tourist." He laughs at himself. "Everything all right?" He sits beside her on the bench.

"Yeah. Mike and Bunny are worried about the weather. They're thinking about flying out tonight."

***

Henri's heart drops to his gut. He looks to the dark sky and back to her. She's radiant despite the disappointment in her eyes.

"She also mentioned staying on for a few more days and waiting out the storm."

He's soaring at the thought. *What a divine intervention.* To get to spend more time with her would be a blessing he didn't deserve, but one he'd readily accept. "I know which I would prefer."

"Me too. But I don't want to be caught in a hurricane either." She's looking up at him, her eyes big and full of worry. He looks at the sky again and back to her.

"Honestly, I don't think it's going to be that bad. There is definitely a storm coming. But in truth, we don't get that many hurricanes. Ever since Katrina people think they happen all the time."

"Oh. I guess I did too." She looks at the sky.

"You and everyone else to the north and west of us." He chuckles and pulls her to his chest. She sighs then pulls away from him, swiping her hair away from her face.

"It's way too hot for snuggling out here," she says, twisting her hair up in a bun. "But you smell amazing, despite it." She laughs, fanning at her chest and neck with her hands.

"Thank you. It's Hové. One of the places I want to show you. It's not far from here. Let's talk on the way." Henri stands and offers his hand. She takes it and rises. They walk in a comfortable silence, her hand in his. Without a breeze, the heat is oppressive. The sky looks more ominous than he let on. It is dark for sure, but not hurricane dark. No matter what the grade of storm coming, he knows what he wants. He wants her to check out of her hotel and stay with him tonight, and every night that she's here. The more the better. "I think you should stay," he says.

"What do you mean? You think it's going to get bad?"

"I don't know about that, but the thought of you staying a little longer, even a day, makes me happy." His heart races and his chest feels funny.

"Well, we want you to be happy, right?" she says with the flat tone she uses when his spoiled nature makes an appearance.

"Ouch."

"What? What did I say?"

"It wasn't what you said, but how you said it."

"Oh, well I'm sorry if my concern for my safety takes precedence over your happiness," she snaps.

Henri finds himself stumbling for words. "That's not what I meant."

"What did you mean?"

"What I mean is…" He swallows hard. "I mean that no matter what the weather holds, I hate the idea of you leaving. If those dark clouds are the key to you staying longer, then so be it. Your safety isn't an issue. Look around you. Business as usual. If there were any real threat, people would be shuttering their windows and closing shops. I'd be ushering you off to the airport as quickly as possible. I believe that Mike is being overly cautious, but if his caution will keep you here, I won't argue."

"What if it has me on a plane tonight?" she asks.

"Then I'll get a seat next to you." They both stop. He can't believe what he said. The idea of following a woman home had never occurred to him. He rarely concerned himself with where they were from, but with Bridgette, he finds himself wondering what her home is like and how many flights to Chicago a man could make in one year.

"I'm sorry, what?"

"I'd book a flight for myself. I'll follow you to Chicago."

Her brow knits. "I don't remember inviting you." She walks away.

For a moment Henri is tempted to let her walk out of his life forever. Her moods are painfully unpredictable, turning in a snap. A thing that would send him running in the other direction with anyone else. But he's drawn to her by something stronger than his wounded ego. There's a light that glows from her, a comfort he finds in her arms that he can't resist. He hurries to follow. He can't let her go.

"I'm sorry, I didn't mean that I would come without your blessing. I only…"

"Look." She stops and turns on her heel. "I like you. I'm enjoying our time together. But this." She gestures between them. "This is an equal proposition. Your entitlement may get you a lot of things, but I'm not one of them." Her words are like daggers. She looks up at him, anger shining in her dark eyes.

He presses his lips together and nods. "I understand." The joy that lives between them is tenuous. A fragile thing that requires tending. Something entirely new to him. His liaisons have always been simple. Straightforward. He's never asked for anything beyond company and physical connection. With Bridgette, he wants more. He wants every part of her. Even the bad. She has no qualms calling him out on his behavior, something he isn't used to. Maybe it's something he needs.

He stands silent, choosing his next words carefully. "I'm sorry," he says slowly. "I didn't mean to assume that you would have me." Her angry eyes soften. "I apologize if that's how it came across. It seems I can't keep my foot out of my mouth when you're around." She pulls a face and gives him a half smile. "Can I be painfully honest?"

"I have a feeling you will be either way," she says with a subtle shake of her head.

"I can't think straight when I'm with you. When I'm not with you, you're the only thing I think about. I know it's presumptuous to believe you feel the same way, but damn if I can't hope you do. You make me crazy, Bridgette. I want to understand you. I want to know you well enough to stop offending you with every other sentence. I want to make you smile and laugh. I haven't felt this way about someone in a long. long time. I don't understand it and it scares the hell out of me."

***

Bridgette looks up at Henri, then away. The pain and honesty in his voice, on his face, is unbearable. She understands every word he says because she feels the same way. It's foolish, though, to feel so much for someone she's only met a day ago. She's seen what happens when a woman jumps into something too good to be true. How many times had her mother told her, "He's the one, baby. The one that's going to take care of us." They never were. Not once did the man her mother hoped would be their hero come through. How could Henri be any different?

This is a sexy affair. A beautiful sensual adventure. Next week it'll be nothing more than a fond memory Yet, all she wants to do is kiss away his pain. To hold him in her arms and reassure him that the feelings are mutual, and to tell him the thought of him joining her on the flight back home set a thousand butterflies loose in her stomach.

"I'm sorry, Henri. Things are moving so fast. It scares me too." She stands on tiptoes and brushes his cheek with a quick kiss. She takes his hand and gives it a squeeze. He looks at their fingers lacing together and smiles. As fiercely protective as she is of her own heart, the idea of breaking his affects her viscerally. "So, tell me about Hové."

"I think you're going to love it. It's a *parfumeur*. The oldest one in New Orleans. It was opened by a Creole woman after the stock market crash. She supported her family throughout the great depression and handed the business down to her daughter in the sixties. It's been in the family for four generations. There are so many scents to choose from and the quality is amazing."

"That's so cool. I bet she was a badass."

"Yeah. They say she traveled the world to learn everything she could about making perfume. It shows in the remarkable scents the store sells."

"I'm going to have to research this lady. It's such a great story."

"Wait 'til you see the place. It's not the original building, but you wouldn't know it. Her family lived above the original shop throughout her life. Now they do again."

"That's too cool."

"Hey," he says, giving her hand a little tug. "I want to spoil you when we get there. I want you to get whatever you'd like." She opens her mouth to protest, but he continues, "It's what I want to do, and you'll hurt my feelings if you say no." She smiles and shakes her head.

Being spoiled isn't something she wants from him. She's sure plenty of women let him, even ask it of him. But she doesn't want to be one of those women. Receiving gifts is not something she enjoys. A little trinket that says *I thought of you* is always fun to get from a loved one, but in her experience, expensive, extravagant gifts come wrapped in demands.

Her dad loved to buy her things. He showered her with gifts and used them to control her. If it didn't work, he'd take them back. Like the puppy he bought her when he remarried, trying to lure her to live with him and the younger version of her mom. When it didn't work, the dog was sent away, and she was heartbroken. Or the car he bought when she was sixteen. When he learned her mom had been driving it, he reported it stolen. Or the men who promised her mother so much over the years, only to leave her worse than they found her. Even her grandparents, whom she loved more than anyone in the world, seemed to remind her always of the sacrifices they had to make for her and her mother.

"I don't know if I'm comfortable with that." She glances his way. He's looking straight ahead.

"You are a rare bird, *cherie*." He sighs.

"Am I?"

"*Oui.*"

"How's that?" she asks, her cheeks warming. In the hours they'd been together she's grown to love him calling her *cherie*. There's something about him speaking French with his accent that's irresistible.

"You are so underwhelmed by my charms."

She scoffs. "Your charms affect me plenty."

"Do they?" He winks.

"Are you fluent?"

"Hmm?"

"In French? You sprinkle in a word here and there. But do you speak fluently?"

"*Oui, ma chere maintenant s'il vous plait laissez-moi vous gater.*"

"That was nice. What did you say?"

"*Amayakasasete kudasai.*"

"What was that?" she asks, impressed. He smiles wide and laughs.

"That was Japanese."

"Show-off," she teases. "You speak three languages then?"

"Four if you count my knack for the Cajun dialect."

"I mean, I feel like I should. Where'd you learn that?"

"They have some of the best music and food out on the bayou."

"Of course, they do." She shakes her head. "But what were you saying?"

"Only what I've been saying all along. I want to spoil you. Look, we're here." He points to the wooden sign above them jutting out from below a wrought-iron balcony. It's pale blue and adorned with a crown.

Bridgette is more excited than she expected to be as they walk through the door. A portrait of the founder looks down on her as she enters, whispering of the history of the business and the women who ran it. The perfumed air is a heavenly mix of sweet, spice, floral, and musk. Wooden cabinets filled with bottles of gleaming golden liquid like an old-world apothecary tower one wall. Glass display cases hold an assortment of jewelry and crystal diffusers, arranged perfectly. All around the shop are little tables offering soaps and candles. It is the loveliest assault on the senses. Henri follows one step behind her as she handles and sniffs everything that catches her eye.

"Let's find your scent, *ma cher*," he says close to her ear, the warmth of his breath raising the tiny hairs on her neck. With his hand on her elbow, he guides her to the counter. She's swept away by his soft voice and gentle touch.

Less than an hour later, Henri gets his way. She leaves Hové with more product than she could possibly use and a signature scent that smells like it was made for her. Henri is smiling down at her with a satisfied grin.

"Thank you," she says, nodding to the bag he's carrying and sniffing her wrist again.

"No, thank you. I know you didn't want to let me buy it all."

"I didn't, but I do appreciate it. It really does smell amazing."

"I look forward to seeing you in nothing else later."

"Nothing but my perfume?" she asks with a dry laugh.

"And maybe this." He hands her the bag his hat came in. She looks in to see the scarf she'd been admiring. Her breath catches in her throat and a small smile plays at the corners of her lips.

"How did you know?" she asks, pulling it out of the bag.

"I saw you looking at them and I chose the one that looked like you." She shakes her head, moved by the attention he pays her, and wonders if his intentions might be as pure as they seem.

"Thank you. It's beautiful." She places it back in the bag and looks at the sky. "I think we might want to head back to the hotel soon."

"I think you're right," he agrees. "But…" He stops walking and pulls at her hand. "Stay with me tonight," he says, smiling down at her, holding on to her fingertips. "At my place. Check out of your room and stay with me." His request hits her harder than it should. How will she ever get on a plane the next morning if she goes with him?

"I don't know. I have to figure out what's happening with Bunny and Mike and our flights." He brings her fingers to his lips and brushes them with a kiss.

"At least consider it. We can watch the storm from my balcony." His eyes crinkle with a playful grin. "Or not."

The thought of spending a night with him in his bed, on his balcony, is overwhelming in the best possible way. She pulls at his hand and starts walking again.

"I will."

Chapter 11

"I got him to agree to stay until Wednesday." Bunny sits on the corner of Bridgette's bed. Henri and Mike are waiting for them in the restaurant downstairs for lunch. "I wanted to talk with you before we made any arrangements. We got flight insurance when we booked the trip so it shouldn't cost anything. Plus, Mike's got a way of getting what he wants from people." She smiles that dreamy smile she wears whenever she mentions his many attributes. Bridgette is beginning to understand where it comes from.

"Henri wants me to stay with him tonight," Bridgette blurts out. "He wants me to pack up my things and leave the hotel for the rest of our time here."

Bunny cocks her head and lifts an eyebrow. "And?"

"I don't know. It seems like a lot. Doesn't it?" Bridgette's heart is banging heavily in her chest while her brain is running a million and one scenarios of how it could all go wrong.

"I don't know. I mean you already fucked him. So, what's the difference between here and there?"

"There's a big difference. Here is a common ground. It's not as personal. If I go there and get all wrapped up in his surroundings, I'm not going to want to leave."

"It's that serious?"

"I don't fucking know. He's infuriating. But also amazing. You know he speaks three languages? I failed Spanish, and he's wooing me in French and Japanese. Like, what the fuck, dude?"

"For real? Damn. That's sexy."

"You're telling me."

They sit in silence on the edge of her bed. Then Bunny asks, "So, what's the problem then?"

"He's the problem. This is the problem." She gestures wildly to the room and the window. "There's like a thousand miles between us, and he seems perfect. Everything I could fall for. But I can't tell you how many times the *perfect man* came into my mother's life. How many nights I spent trying to sleep while my mom shared her bed with monsters. My dad was the best of them, and that wasn't by much." Bridgette stares blindly into her past, tears wetting her eyes, and sighs. "I swear he's incapable of love." She closes her eyes, pushing the pain of the memories deep down. "Let's say Henri *is* perfect. That he's everything he seems to be. Then what? Give up my life to be with him? I mean look what happened with you. One week with Mike and you were gone."

"It was different with us. We had a history."

"I know. And we don't. I know so little about him." Bridgette throws herself back on the bed with a groan. "Fuck," she says with a heavy sigh.

"I say go for it. I know I'm supposed to be responsible and tell you to choose the safer option. But that would make me a hypocrite. Besides, what've you got to lose?"

"My fucking mind."

"I know this is nothing like what happened with me and Mike, but I have a feeling you'll regret not doing it."

"You think so?"

"Yep. If meeting Henri was something you could forget about or walk away from easily, you would have already. If you don't like someone's energy, you walk away, no questions. You must like his. I've never seen you this way."

Bridgette looks at her friend and sits up. "Really?" She tries to think of another guy who made her feel the way Henri does.

"You really need me to point that out? When was the last time you fucked on the first date?"

"It was our second."

"Sorry. When was the last time you fucked on the second date?"

Bridgette squints at her friend. They both know the answer is never. She learned early on to always keep her guard up. Watching her mom give her love so freely over the years to one asshole after another taught Bridgette to keep it close and keep it safe. The only man in her life she could count on no matter what was her grandpa. He had proved that time and again, rescuing her and her mom from more than one bad situation. That Henri slid past those defenses so easily baffles her. She loves his smile, and the way it crinkles his eyes. And the way he holds the tips of her fingers. He seems concerned about her and he's patient. But is she seeing what she wants to see? Is he as genuine and kind as he seems, or is she blinded by his handsome charm?

"Hmmm?" Bunny asks, tilting her head.

"You're right." Bridgette shakes the thoughts away. "He's different. But I barely know him."

"What better way to get to know him?"

"You really are a terrible influence."

Bunny grins. "If you ask Mike, he'd say I'm the worst. I swear that man must have done nothing but work before we found each other. The things I do to keep him in bed on the weekends." She giggles. "Otherwise he would start building something or fixing something or making plans to build or fix something. He's unstoppable." She sighs and Bridgette shakes her head. "You should hear the things I have to do to keep him here for a couple more days." Bunny's cheeks color noticeably.

Bridgette sucks her teeth and stands. "Thank you. I guess."

"No thanks necessary. Two more nights in this hotel with that man is fine by me. You gave me an excuse to push for it."

"Well, you're welcome then," Bridgette says slowly. "I guess I'm going to do this." She begins gathering her things from around the room. "Come what may. Right?" She swallows the lump in her throat and ignores the nervous trembles in her gut.

"Come what may," Bunny agrees with a soft smile and dreamy look in her eye.

***

"So, what *do* you do?" Mike asks, leveling his cold blue stare on Henri. They're sitting at a table for four, sipping beers, waiting for Bridgette and Bunny. Henri notices the black stains in the creases of Mike's thick fingers as they wrap around the dark bottle. He's a working man for sure. The kind Henri's dad would call the "salt of the earth" or "backbone of America." Henri looks at his manicured hands, which have never seen what Mike would call a real day's work. Henri laughs at himself and takes another swig. They couldn't be more different. But he knows how Bridgette feels about Mike, which makes earning his respect all the more important. Henri feels like he's meeting her father or brother for the first time.

"I make a lot of music. I help local musicians get in front of the right people. But, mostly, I spend my parents' money." He scratches the back of his neck and swipes at his hair. Mike blinks and takes a long drink.

"Hm," is all he says.

Henri cringes internally, wondering where Bridgette is. At least Bunny seems to like him. "I'll be the first to admit I've lived a charmed life. But I do my best to help my community. You drop a hundred-dollar bill in a street musician's case and you've made their day."

"It's the little things," Mike says with sarcasm not lost on Henri.

"Say what you will, but I have helped a lot of folks, and music is the lifeblood of this town." They sit in awkward silence, watching out the window, looking toward the door for Bridgette and Bunny.

"So, what do you think of the weather?" Mike asks, nodding to the dark clouds.

"It's gonna storm for sure, but I don't think it'll be too bad."

"Good. Looks like we'll be here for a couple more nights either way. Amanda was really pushing to stay. I don't think it has anything to do with the weather though. She loves it here."

"I'm glad. This is a magical city. What do you think?"

"It's a great place for a vacation, but I'm not really the city type. I'm hoping to check out the swamps before we leave now that we're extending our stay."

"I know a few great places you could go," Henri offers, pleased to find a comfortable topic. He knows a man like Mike is unimpressed with Henri's genteel existence. But Henri has knowledge that Mike doesn't, which seems to be of value. "I have a few friends who do private tours. They're much better than the group ones you'd book downtown. Plus, they feed you." Mike's expression shifts and he acts interested. "Some of the best food you'll have here."

"I'm going to want those numbers," Mike says, finishing his beer. He looks around for their waiter, and his eyes light up. Henri follows his gaze. Bridgette and Bunny enter the restaurant. They watch in silence as the two lovely creatures approach the table.

Henri stands to pull Bridgette's chair out. Mike smiles as Bunny wraps her arms around him, planting a kiss on his face. Henri notes the change in his demeanor when she's around. How he softens.

Bridgette takes her seat. Henri gives her shoulder a gentle squeeze before he sits. She smells amazing. The perfume from Hové blends beautifully with her natural scent. His stomach does a flip at the thought that he has three more nights with her.

Chapter 12

With her bags at her feet, Bridgette stands on the porch, soaked to the bone. Their Lyft pulls away into the haze of heavy rain. The rhythm of the giant drops on the roof plays as hard and fast as her heartbeat. She can't believe she's doing this. The spontaneity the night before had made everything so much easier. Pulling him into her room, falling into bed with him. She hadn't had hours to think about it. Hadn't shared a long, awkward car ride from the hotel with him watching her, his hand holding hers while his knee bounced nervously.

Henri smiles at her, oblivious, as he pushes the door open and carries her bags into the house. Bones trots out to meet her, his big black eyes shining with excitement. She kneels to scratch his head despite her dripping clothes. Thunder rumbles in the distance, and a gust of wind chills her skin. She feels like a child again, remembering standing on the front porch of a strange house on a stormy night. Her mom is there, fawning over the man Bridgette met only once before. She had known even then, at the age of seven, that he hadn't bargained for a child when he asked her mom to move in. He'd made no attempt to hide his annoyance at the presence of an awkward, nervous Bridgette. Lightning flashes across the New Orleans sky, jarring her from another bad memory.

Bones runs inside. Henri reappears, his lightweight shirt clinging to the fine definition of his upper body. He steps beside her, offering his hand. She takes it, stands, and her cold, wet dress clings to her like the memory of that night.

"Let's get inside and get dry," he says, leading her into the house. Her tongue is thick and heavy in her mouth as she searches for her voice.

The smell of freshly oiled floors is overcome by musty wetness as the old house drinks in the rain. It's as beautiful as it had been when she first saw it, yet different. With the shutters closed up tight, there's no natural light. The bright and lively sitting room has an altogether new quality. Instead of the colorful throw pillows and accent pieces, her eyes are drawn to an iron sculpture in the corner, a small, grinning naked man with eyes and teeth cut out like a jack-o-lantern. In one hand he holds a spear, in another his own stubby phallus.

Standing candelabras are set along the walls in measured intervals with large black candles that have never been lit. There are some in the fireplace as well, arranged beautifully with fresh white wicks. The painting that had seemed so playful with its rainbow menagerie and bright foliage reveals its more sinister side. The animals grin with sharpened teeth. The little people, merely a handful of brushstrokes, brandish weapons as they dance around the flames that spread throughout the landscape. Everything is burning. The incandescent lights above are warm, however dim.

"You all right?" Henri asks from the stairway. He's standing with his hand on the banister, his wet shirt open. Bridgette's gaze shifts from the painting to his face, then his bare chest. He's calmer now. The nervous energy is hers alone. "You're shivering." He closes the distance between them.

"It's cold," she squeaks as his warm hands rest on her shoulders, wiping away the rain. She feels helpless, childlike. Her thoughts bounce around her mind as she looks into his eyes. His eyebrows raise as he runs his hands over her arms.

"You sure you're okay?" He holds both of her hands. There's a comfortable distance between them. Bones passes through it and circles them, tongue out, tail wagging.

"Yeah. It's…" She looks at her hands in his, down to the dog prancing around them, then back into Henri's eyes. "It's different without the shutters open. The storm is pretty wild. I'm adjusting, I guess. I need a minute," she says, nodding her head toward the stairs.

"Take all the time you need." He lets go of her hands and steps away from the stairway. "I'll take your bags up."

Ascending the stairway, she doesn't look back. The hall at the top is darker than the rest of the house. Unencumbered as she is, she feels the weight of the bags she'd fumbled with that night so many years ago, along with the weight of the cold stare of Mom's new hero. Bridgette had tripped and watched with fear as her few belongings tumbled down the stairs, knocking over a vase. It shattered when it hit the floor. His rage had been so immense, she could feel it still. Now, her heart beats as wildly as if he were standing at the foot of the stairs where her mother soothed him with her soft, passive voice.

Light spills from the bedroom door, doing little to calm her. She heads to it and into the master suite that she'd only glimpsed in passing the last time she was here; she tries to focus on the bed with its thick golden blankets. Or the plush jewel-toned pillows, piled high with Moroccan flair. The shutters are open to the balcony. Bridgette watches through the window as the rain falls in heavy gray sheets. She's trapped. The wind pulls and whips through the plants. Thunder rumbles again, seeming to shake the entire house. She turns to the door behind her. It's open to the bathroom. With the flip of a switch she's surprised how bright white and meticulously clean it is. Velvety soft towels in gray and cream sit in a stack on the shelf beside the sink. She takes one and towels her hair roughly and runs it over her chilled, damp skin. Facing the mirror, she asks herself, *What are you doing here?* There's a light knock at the door, and she jumps, remembering the slamming doors and shouting, the quiet murmur of her mother's voice through the wall as she attempted to quiet an out-of-control man.

"Hey, I've got your bags out here," Henri says through the door. "I'm going to change real quick, then I'll be downstairs in the back room." His voice is gentle, nothing like the raging brute from her memory.

"Thanks. I'll be down in a bit." She drapes the thick towel over her shoulders before slipping out of her wet dress. Goosebumps spread over her legs, and her heart is racing at the idea of Henri on the other side of the door. He's a stranger. He could be anyone. For all that they've shared over the last two days, she doesn't know a thing about him. Her heart thumps against her ribcage.

"Oh no," she whimpers, feeling the all-too-familiar beginnings of a panic attack. She wraps the towel tightly around her naked body. Her numb skin is welcome compared to the hot turmoil churning in her belly and chest. Her blood rushes in her ears. *Stranger.* Her stomach churns and tightens. Her throat closes on her breaths. The brightness of the room fades as blackness crowds her peripheral. She's shaking as tears run from her eyes. *What are you doing here?*

Hugging herself tightly, she paces the large bathroom, barely seeing her surroundings. The overwhelming reality that Henri is a stranger and she's in a strange place means she's trapped here.

That night comes back. How she had hidden in the hall bathroom waiting for her mother to find her, to tell her everything would be okay. But she never came. Bridgette waited there until the house grew still then crept into her new bedroom. There had been no good-night hugs or kisses, no sleep tight. Only a small bed in a stark room with her bags on the floor. She'd cried herself to sleep, clinging to the blanket her grandma had given her earlier that night.

Pacing Henri's lovely bathroom, she thinks of her hotel room and longs for the safe space. Then she remembers the storm raging outside and how it separates her from that safety.

Her breaths are coming fast and heavy as she paces, feeling more trapped with each frantic step. "Find five things," she says to herself, voice trembling. "Five things." She lowers onto the side of the tub, shaking. *My feet.* She focuses on her feet, her red toenails against the white tiles. *The grout.* She follows the light gray lines as they run to and from her feet and across, back and forth. *My dress.* It's there in a rumpled pile on the floor, dark and soaked with rain. *The door.* It's tall and white with a window above it, wavering in her blurred vision. *The knob.* Shining brass, reflecting the overhead light.

She takes five long slow breaths, steadying herself. "Four things," she says and closes her eyes. She listens to her own breath as it expands and contracts in her lungs. Then, the rain on the roof pattering its heavy cadence. She sways and breathes deep. The wind as it sings its angry song. She reaches for the faucet and turns on the water. It runs with a calm and fluid contrast to the rain.

"Three things." She sighs again and holds her fingertips under the cool water. Her heart rate is slowing. Her peripheral vision returns. She feels the cool tile under her feet and breathes again. Then, she sinks into the softness of the towel around her frame. It's warm and comforting.

"Two things," she says with another deep breath. First, there's the smell of the water running from old pipes. Then, bringing her wrist to her nose, she inhales the scent of her new perfume. It takes her back to the shop, to the street afterward with Henri looking so pleased. As she starts to settle into calming, she's aware of the acrid taste of stress in her mouth.

"One thing." She leans over the tub to drink from the polished brass faucet. The water is cool with a hint of must. Bridgette slouches, her nerves raw.

She admires the clawfoot tub. It's deep and sparkling clean with the cold water still running. Her chilled skin is sticky and uncomfortable. She remembers her bag from Hové. Surely Henri brought that up with the rest of her things. And he did say to take all the time she needed. Turning on the hot water, she plugs the tub and tests the temperature. She crosses to the door, listening before she opens it. Nothing but quiet on the other side. She cracks it open and peeks out. There's no one there. Her bags are sitting no more than a foot from the door, the package from Hové on top. The faint sound of music drifts up the stairs.

She takes her things and closes the door behind her. As the tub fills, she sorts through her clothes for something comfortable to wear. She takes a ragged breath and selects a delightfully calming scented bath bomb. As she drops it in the tub, she lowers into the warm fizzing water and lets herself melt into the sensation.

Her anxiety continues to whisper in her mind, mapping all the things that could go wrong. All the reasons she shouldn't be where she is. As the bath bomb bubbles and rolls at her feet, she asks herself *What in the world am I doing in this man's bathtub?* Her phone pings a message notification. It's Henri as if on cue.

Heard the tub running. Enjoy your bath. I'll order some delivery for dinner. Anything I should avoid?

The normalcy of the text settles and centers her and she appreciates his thoughtfulness.

I eat anything. LOL Thanks. This tub is magnificent.
Glad you like it. Take your time.

She places her phone on the shelf beside the tub and slides deeper into the water, taking in several slow, deep breaths. *Can't believe I'm here in this beautiful bathroom, in this luxurious tub with a thoughtful, tender, handsome stranger waiting on me.*

These things don't happen to people like me.

***

"What do you think, Bones?" Henri asks the dog. He lifts his fuzzy snout from its place on Henri's knee and looks at him with his quirky dog expression. "I like her," he says. Bones lays his head back down. Henri relaxes into the couch and listens to the music. He's glad she's made herself at home, though he wishes he were there in the bathroom with her. He could pull up a chair and sit beside her while she bathed. Or sit at a distance and watch as she soaked and washed herself. The thought of her rosebud nipples peeking out of soapy water is almost too much. He's less than patient as he imagines her smooth skin wet and slippery. What he wouldn't give to join her in that tub, to feel that beautiful slippery skin against his.

Another time, maybe. She seemed upset when we came in. She needs time to relax. To get comfortable. Don't wanna fuck this up.

He busies himself with ordering dinner. Lucky enough, his favorite service delivers from Baccanal. He places an order for the finest charcuterie spread they offer along with two bottles of Spanish wine. One a light, almost sweet red. The other deep, rich, and full bodied. He adds some chocolate cake and a berry torte to the order and sits back satisfied. The spread will look perfect on the coffee table. They can sit, smoke, eat, and make love all night and not even leave this room.

But that's not what he wants. No, he wants to see her in every room in every way possible. He wants her on every piece of furniture, on his counter in the kitchen, in his room, on the balcony. He wants to fill his empty house with the song of her laughter. To make her so comfortable and happy she never wants to leave. Or at least so she can't wait to return. "What's she doing to me, boy?" he asks the half-asleep dog. Bones shifts closer to him, nuzzling his hand. Henri looks to the tin ceiling tiles, absently scratching Bones' ears.

Any other night he would be in his studio making music, editing tracks to create the best result. But it didn't seem right to be up there now. He wanted to give her the space she clearly needed. She confuses him. She seems bold and fragile at the same time. When they got here, she seemed truly distraught. He replays all their moments together as he sits and waits. From when he first saw her in the shop, looking so innocent and sweet, to the night she pulled him into her room and held him like a goddess. When he watched her ascend the stairs, soaked to the bone, she was distant, almost fearful. He remembers her trepidation that afternoon as they talked of the coming storm. Many people fear extreme weather. In and of itself, it's not odd, but he feels it's something more.

Time passes slowly at a pace reserved for the impatient. Henri sits fixated on Bridgette. In a moment of weakness, he pulls up Google on his phone and searches her name. Bridgette O'Hare. Being a common name, he has to scroll quite a way to find her. Through various social media platforms, he discovers her business sites, O'h Design along with O'Hare Photography.

He admires the artistic quality of her photos, the way she captures the beauty of her subject. From broken buildings to newborn babies and everything in between. He wonders what she might do with her camera here in the city he loves so dearly as he scrolls through the various files of her work. Inside the senior portraits folder he finds a feisty-looking redhead trying too hard to look cool in her punk rock clothes, holding a barely used skateboard.

Then, with all the cruelty memories possess, he remembers a young girl with a skateboard. Dottie Pearl had been his absolute favorite thing about life. In his sixteen-year-old mind, she was perfection. She lived by the river in a small house with a big family. She wore oversize jeans and tiny shirts. She styled her short dark hair with the cheapest, terribly scented gel. It was stiff to touch and really quite awful. But he loved the way she wore it along with her dark red lipstick. He first saw her on a half-pipe.

He and some friends had ventured to the worst part of town, to a derelict building full of fellow punk-ass kids. The music blared from a crappy CD player perched on a broken wall. Dottie was there, among the best of them, practically flying. No pads, no helmet, only her body and the board. For teenage Henri it was love at first sight. "She's a beast," he recalls his friend saying to him as his jaw hung open. "Careful though, she's got teeth too." His friends laughed at his expense. But he didn't care. She was the most amazing thing on two legs and four wheels that he had ever seen.

He was a terrible skater. But he had the best drugs and the most booze so he fit in fine. Within weeks he was a permanent fixture in the building. They called him Richie Rich. He didn't mind. Dottie called him Henri. She didn't smoke weed, but she drank like a fish and couldn't get enough of her Marlboro Reds. They would often go for walks along the river. She would lament about her family and the tiny house they occupied. She wanted to go west to California.

Claimed she would live under a bridge and be happier for it. Henri had little to offer in those moments, except for the promise to go with her. They had a song. "The Way" by Fastball. Whenever they heard it, they would talk about leaving. They never made it.

Henri's heart aches, unsure why these memories won't leave him be. He'd been at peace with it all for so long. Barely thinking of Dottie, and never thinking of that night. Why now? He pushes the pain deep down. Brushes the memories from the surface back to where they belong.

Bridgette is here, and she leaves no room for ghosts.

Chapter 13

"I'll be honest with you," Bridgette says over the rim of her wineglass. The spread before her is sumptuous. Cured meats, French cheeses, fresh baked bread, artesian crackers, delicious sauces, gourmet jams, and pickled vegetables with dried fruits and nuts sprinkled throughout. Every taste is a new flavor experience. She takes a hearty swallow of the dry, oaky wine before continuing. "I don't know what the fuck I'm doing here." She laughs, the second glass of wine lubricating her candor.

"I'm sorry. I don't think I follow." Henri smiles at her from behind his glass.

"This is the craziest thing I've ever done." She places her glass on the table and reaches for more bread and meat. "I can't believe I came home with you."

"I hope you aren't regretting your choice." His statement carries the weight of concern. She looks at him while chewing the crusty bread, contemplating her response.

"You're used to getting what you want, aren't you?" she asks.

He places his glass on the table and leans back into the couch. Bones is lying on the floor, quietly watching their every move, patiently waiting for a scrap to fall or be offered.

"I am," Henri says without defense.

"I'm not."

"What do you mean by that?" he asks, curiosity on his brow.

Bridgette looks away from him to Bones, then over the spread. She's sitting with her legs and feet tucked under her in lounge pants. There's a natural comfort to it all. As though they've done this a hundred times before. It's confusing how right it feels.

"Things don't come easy for me. They never have. I wasn't born into a world that fell at my feet." Henri flinches. "I've got student loan debt, a broken family, and a day job. This is a vacation for me while it's every day of your life." He's silent as Bridgette spews words between them, building a wall around herself. "I don't know if I want you or if I want to be you." She ends with a dry laugh to cover her discomfort at such blunt honesty.

Henri sits silent, watching her. She tears a small piece of bread from the slice in her hand and pops it in her mouth, looking away from his steady gaze.

"I don't think you want to be me," he says, his voice flat, lacking the playful cadence that she's come to adore. "My life may be charmed, there's really no denying that. But I've had struggles. I've had experiences I wouldn't wish on anyone. I've paid my dues. Maybe not in the traditional sense. Maybe not the way most people do, but it hasn't been all playboy parties and jet-setting around the world."

"Could've fooled me."

"It's the mask I wear. I'm more comfortable behind it. Like you and burlesque."

"Excuse me?" She shifts in her seat, tossing the last of her bread to Bones.

"When you're on stage, you're wearing a mask. The mask of a dancer. Hell, your mask has its own name. You're Baby La Loop up there. To anyone who doesn't know you, it's all that you are. All you'll ever be. But under that, off stage, every other moment of your life, you're Bridgette. The mask you wear as Bridgette for your family is different from the one you wear for Bunny. You wear a different mask for your grandma than you do your grandpa."

Bridgette sits quietly and reaches for her wine. "The thing about all these masks is you aren't even aware when you change them. Take Mike for instance. With me he presents an intimidating nature. A man of little words not to be trifled with or stepped on. He threatens destruction to anyone who would harm someone he loves." Henri reaches for his glass and goes on. "That's you by the way. He's exceptionally protective. That's his mask for you. Big brother. Protector." Bridgette smiles at the thought. "Then Bunny enters the room and he's a different man completely, consumed by her. A devoted champion to his queen." Bridgette nods and laughs at the truth of it all.

"That's for sure," she agrees with a relaxed laugh. "So, what type of mask are you wearing now?" She tilts her chin.

"Whatever one will make you fall head over heels in love with me." He smiles and finishes his wine, reaching for the open bottle. With a quick gesture, he offers to fill hers. She accepts and considers his comment with a smile. Her heart jumps at his words. How easy it would be to fall for him. But still, trust doesn't come easy for her. Letting people in is difficult.

"I enjoy this mask. But that might be the wine talking."

"Then let it talk," he says with a lift of his brow and a smile to die for.

There's a long pause between them. Bridgette measures the distance, contemplating all the masks they've worn, wondering about his past, the darkness he's alluded to but hasn't offered to share. She sips her wine and listens to the low music, remembering the storm that's raging outside and the panic she'd felt earlier. The trembling woman in the tub seemed a world away. *Me without a mask.*

Then she speaks quickly. "It shouldn't be *this* easy, though."

"Why is that? Why can't it be?"

"I don't know. That's what I was asking myself in the tub earlier. Why can't I embrace this for all its ease? Why am I fighting?"

"This is fighting?" he asks with a small gesture of his hand.

"It's internal," she says, quickly looking away.

"Well, *ma cher*, internal battles are part of life. We all have them. The trick is not letting them get in the way of what you want."

"What is it that you want?" she whispers.

"I thought that was painfully obvious," he says, blinking slowly.

Bridgette's cheeks warm, and her stomach does a pleasant flip. She smiles from behind the wineglass and takes one more hearty sip before placing it on the table. A hint of berry sweetness lingers on her tongue.

Henri follows her lead. They sit, still, their bodies angled toward one another.

She notices how the distance between them has shrunk throughout their conversation. One tiny shift at a time. Bridgette maps his face. His thick hair, normally so perfectly placed, is roughed and unkempt. The way the plain white t-shirt hugs his frame is sexier than anything else she's seen him in. She breathes in deep. The air smells of him, light and intoxicating.

He reaches out to her hand on the cushion between them, resting his on hers. A rush of excitement runs the length of her arm. The tiny hairs on her scalp rise. Her nipples tingle. She turns her palm to his.

The sensation builds as their fingers play then lace together. Henri grins, his eyes crinkling, teeth flashing white. Bridgette tugs at his hand, and he closes the distance between them.

His lips touch hers with soft urgency, tender and slow but calling to every cell in her body. His fingers caress her hand with the same gentle demand. She lies back, and he follows her lead. He's beside her and above her. As they sink into the couch, his hand runs from her hip to her rib cage and back down over her tank top. She runs her fingers over his chest, relishing in his taut frame.

Sneaking her hand under his shirt, she explores the smooth, warm skin of his back. He responds in kind, slipping his hand under her shirt, resting it on her ribs, his knuckle brushing the side of her breast. An enticing tingle spreads from his hand.

She longs for more, arching her back in a silent plea. He answers, cupping her breast fully with a small squeeze, then the lightest of tweaks on her swollen, tender nipple. A small gasp escapes her lips, and she feels a chuckle in his chest as his kisses leave her mouth, following the line of her jaw to the base of her ear then down her neck.

He rolls his finger and thumb around her nipple, teasing it to full attention. She drops her head back, exposing her neck. His lips travel the length of it, up and down, painfully slow. Every kiss stoking the already burning fire within. As his breath tickles her collarbone, she tugs up at the hem of his shirt. He shifts away and they pull themselves out of their shirts. The reunion of their skin is beautiful as he pulls her into a one-armed embrace.

He's warm, hard, and smooth. His free hand moves on her exposed body as his lips find hers with excruciatingly soft, tender little kisses that tease her to the brink. She flicks her tongue out quickly, testing his desire. He lets out a small groan. She pulls at his bottom lip with her teeth then clutches his head in both hands, pulling him into a deep, crushing kiss. He groans again. His excitement evident against her thigh.

She runs one hand over his shoulder, down his long, lean forearm, and holds it there. Taut muscles pull and shift. He's like candy and she can't get enough. Smooth skin, toned muscles. His back is a playground, silky and irresistible. She slips her fingers under the waistband of his pants. The full, sculpted cheek of his ass begs to be squeezed. She boldly answers the call. A moan rumbles from deep in his chest. He pulls her closer with both arms, sliding one knee between her legs. She rocks against it, pleasure coursing through her.

They sink farther into the couch, hands and lips dancing with surprising familiarity. Bridgette's body responds to his skilled touch and gentle urgency. The way he touches with patience and hunger at the same time. Her head falls back and his lips trail down her throat and shoulders. She sighs, her eyes fluttering open. Bones is there, his face inches from hers. He's lying obediently, his head cocked to one side, ears twitching, as he lets out a long, high-pitched whine. Henri looks up. Bridgette's skin chills at the absence of his attention.

"Go on, Bones," he half whispers to the dog. Bones sits up, looking nervously from Henri to the table full of food with another whimper. His tail thumps once, then twice. "Go on," Henri says with a bit more force, waving at him with his free hand. The dog shifts toward the meat-leaden table and blinks at his master.

Henri's forehead falls to Bridgette's bare chest. "Jesus," he says with a heavy sigh, his voice muffled by her breast. Bridgette places a hand on either cheek, tilting his face to hers. His dark eyes shine with desire and good humor. A warmth glows in her chest and spreads across her face in a full smile. She giggles at the predicament, mostly Henri's. Though she's throbbing with desire, she'd been left longing more than she would like to admit by unskilled lovers. Henri, on the other hand, seems less prepared to be left hanging.

"I'll help you put this away," she says, wiggling out from beneath him and reaching for her shirt. "I think poor Bones is afraid of doing something he'll regret." She laughs and stands up, patting the dog on the head. Then she plucks a piece of meat from the tabletop. Bones takes it gently, wagging his tail. "You're a good boy, aren't you?" she sings, scratching his ears, wanting desperately to be back in Henri's arms.

***

Henri watches Bridgette lavish her love and attention on the dog. Henri's taken, as he has been since he first laid eyes on her. Her essence, her light, is irresistible. He sits up and waits for his own aching discomfort to pass, surveying the food before him. He'd laid it out in a way that would be easy enough to clean up. *Damn Bones.* Henri couldn't fault the dog. He whimpered and whined, trying to stay on his best behavior. It worked. She's hand-feeding him and cooing in his ear. Henri's rushing blood settles. He stands and takes the first platter in his hand, then another. Bridgette does the same and follows him.

Was she looking for a way out? he wonders as he heads to the kitchen. Bridgette follows with Bones close behind. His claws clicking on the floor. *She was into it.* He felt her desire. She drops off her platters and leaves silently. Bones stays at Henri's feet, tongue out, tail wagging. Standing there looking at the sweet hound, Henri is questioning his moves and whether he'd pushed her when she wasn't ready. He'd thought self-torture like this was behind him. He should have never brought her home. He should've stayed at the hotel with her. But he couldn't. Bones needed him. "Way to show your appreciation, boy," Henri mumbled as he wraps the first platter.

"What's that?" Bridgette asks as she enters the room with the two untouched desserts. Her hair is smooth and sleek in a low side ponytail, and her cheeks are still flushed. Her nipples are peaked under the thin fabric of her shirt.

"Talking to the dog," Henri says with a glance her way.

"What's he saying?" She steals a slice of salami from the platter before he covers it with plastic. She takes a bite and throws the rest to Bones.

"That he would have happily helped clean up."

"I'm sure he would have." She scratches his head again. "He was trying so hard to be good."

"He was," Henri agrees as he wraps another platter, stealing glances her way every chance he can.

"I'll go get the rest." She leaves again, and he watches her walk away. The sway of her hips in the baggy lounge pants, the soft pat of her bare feet on the floor. He can't wait to be back in the living room with her. To pick up where they left off.

Bones whimpers again. Henri shoots a look his way and considers kicking him out for the evening. He could sleep on the porch for one night. Thunder rumbles and lightning flashes outside, reminding Henri of the storm. "You're lucky," he grumbles at his four-legged roommate.

Bridgette returns with the last platter, weighed down with jars and dishes, munching happily on a pickle. She sets everything down and pulls up a stool to the breakfast bar, her fingers fishing around in the jar for another pickle. Henri's heart skips at the sight. In that moment, he understands the ease she'd been talking about. In all his adult life he couldn't recall this level of comfort with another person. Since he got on that flight to Japan as a boy, he's been alone. His parents sent him away. His siblings never really cared to know him. His great-grandma had been angry and aloof. In all his travels and all his liaisons, he'd never known this feeling. His chest tightens.

"What?" Bridgette asks, her hand over her mouth as she chews and swallows, her eyes wide.

"Nothing." Henri quickly busies himself with the food.

"You were looking at me funny."

"I spaced out," he said, waving one hand in the air.

"Hmm." She eyes him suspiciously then shifts her gaze to Bones. "I always wanted a dog," she says, smiling at the mutt.

"Yeah? I didn't take you for an animal lover." He slides the last tray in the fridge.

She grins as she plucks olives out of a dish and pops them in her mouth, watching Bones watch him. "He worships you."

"I don't know about that. He likes to eat. I feed him."

"No, it's more than that. Look at the way he looks at you. You saved him and he knows it."

Henri looks down at Bones. His shining black eyes and crooked face look up with his goofy dog smile. He wags his curly tail. A small lump forms in Henri's throat as he remembers how truly empty his house was before Bones came crawling out of the back trashcan. "I don't know who saved who," he says, clearing his throat and looking at her with a quick smile. "We appreciate each other." He tilts his head toward the living room. "Should we get back to our wine?" he asks, trying not to sound too eager.

"Maybe one more glass." She gives him a suggestive smile then stands and heads out of the kitchen. Henri watches as she moves with fluid grace though the doorway into the darkened hallway.

He looks down at Bones. "You, stay," he says with quiet force, pointing down. Bones gives a little whimper, then lies down, his head on his paws. "Good boy." Henri pulls the door closed behind him with a soft click.

A myriad of emotions swell in his chest as he follows Bridgette to the living room. He'd never thought of himself as lonely, not in his adult life. He'd always been independent, content in the choices he made to live the bachelor's life. He'd ignored his family's pleas that he settle down long enough that eventually, they stopped saying anything about it. He'd pushed away any woman who attempted a connection beyond him spoiling her in exchange for her company. He rarely brought them home, content to keep them at arm's length. He usually chose them well, women with the same agenda. Women who happily wore their own masks while accepting his.

Bridgette was different. She didn't care about his masks or his money. She wanted to know who he was without it all.

Moreover, he wanted to show her.

It scared the hell out of him.

Chapter 14

Gotta stop with the wine, Bridgette tells herself. The first bottle is empty. The second sits beside it half full. It's fruity and almost too sweet, but still delicious. Every sip leaves her thirsty for the next. Their words float in clouds around them, hanging comfortably in the air with no linear track to their conversation. A story from her childhood leads to one from his adventures overseas. Then a particularly funny anecdote from that reminds her of something from her time performing on the road with Burlesque A la Mode. They share their experiences in a delightful volley. Random memories surface. Bridgette ignores the bad ones, choosing instead to share the happier snippets of her life, painting the picture she wants him to see.

"I'm not really a drinker," she says, topping off his glass.

"Oh?" Henri raises a brow.

"Whatever." Bridgette laughs, leaning back into the couch, wine sloshing out of her overfilled glass. It runs over her fingers and down the back of her hand, staining her skin. "Oops." She giggles, switching her glass to her other hand and sucking at the spilled wine. "I told you, I'm not a drinker." She sits forward to place the glass on the table. "I should really stop."

"No shame in being a lightweight," he teases, placing his glass on the table as well.

"I'm definitely that." She wipes her sticky hand on her pant leg. "With booze that is. Used to think I could smoke anyone under the table until I smoked some of your weed. You probably fly that shit in from Amsterdam."

"Nope. I've got a local guy. He loves what he does and it shows."

"Too true." Bridgette laughs at herself, remembering how her first hit of his weed had felt.

"Have you ever done a dab?" he asks, sitting up and pulling the drawer under the table open.

"I haven't." She scoots closer to him, curious.

"You've heard of them though?" he asks, pulling out what looks like a tall, thin bong, a small blowtorch, something that looks like a dentist's tool, and a small glass jar.

"Yeah, but I never had the opportunity."

"Would you like to?" He spreads a towel on the tabletop and reaches for a glass of water from the side table. Bridgette examines the instruments he's laid out. They look familiar enough. He pours water into the bong-like apparatus, then, unscrews the top of the jar. The room is instantly filled with a familiar, pungent odor. He hands it to her. She sniffs at the sticky looking golden gel in the bottom. "This is the wax," he says as he reaches for the jar and the dental pick. He scoops a small amount onto the end of it and balances it over the lid.

"This is already too complicated." Bridgette laughs and watches with interest.

"Just wait. It's worth it," he says, reaching for the small blowtorch. He lights it and starts heating what would be the bowl. He cuts off the torch and drops a small glass sleeve over the bowl. Then, he grabs the pick and rests it inside the sleeve, on the bowl. He inhales like he would a regular bowl and sits back, offering Bridgette the pick as smoke billows around him.

"Okay…" She takes the pick and places it to the bowl. Nothing happens.

"You've got to heat it again," he explains, handing her the torch.

"I didn't see torches in my future when I agreed to come home with you."

"Here, I'll heat it." He pulls the sleeve off and runs the torch over the bowl. After a bit he replaces the sleeve and makes room for her. Bridgette lowers the pick to the hot glass and inhales deeply. It's hot, fire in her lungs, hot. She lets out her breath and starts coughing. Her mind races as she watches the cloud of smoke swirl around her face.

Oh shit. She's sure she'll be higher than she's ever been. "I think I'm going to regret that." She wipes spit from her chin with the back of her hand and places the pick on the table.

Her face tingles, her skin feels hot. A sheen of sweat coats her. She tries to focus on Henri's face as he takes another hit, but the air feels thick around her. The music slows. The tempo, the words, the beat are all off. He lays the stick down and turns to face her. She sees his eyes, his smile, his whole face, but not at once. Her focus is limited.

As his eyes crinkle the music fades. While his smile flashes, his eyes seem to disappear. Behind him, the room is somehow sharp and hazy at the same time. She closes her eyes and sinks into the soft cushions while the music finds its rhythm. Her skin cools. Her heart slows. Her mouth feels like a dry sponge. Her eyes flutter open. Henri appears beside her, his brow knit, his face full of concern but clear as can be. Now the music is playing at its proper pace.

"Are you okay?"

"Yeah." She breathes, unsure of her voice. "That hits hard." She chuckles and shifts to sit up. "I need to drink something. Talk about cottonmouth." Henri reaches for her wineglass and passes it her way. The wine is like syrup on her tongue, much thicker and far sweeter than it had been before. She rolls a small amount around her mouth before swallowing it. The syrupy sweetness moves down her throat slowly, seeping into every part of her. With her eyes closed she takes a heartier drink. It finishes with the sharp bitterness of alcohol. She winces and places the glass on the table. "Could I have some water?" Henri is up before she finishes the sentence.

Alone, she searches for something to focus on. Without an anchor, she's sure she'll float away. Above her, the tin-plated ceiling offers plenty to see, shapes and patterns galore. She follows the lines in each tile like a maze, marveling at the intricate designs. The bright red walls would be garish anywhere else, but in this room with its dark drapes, tin ceiling, and leather wainscoting they blend perfectly. It's a room designed to shut out the world. To forget anything else exists.

Henri appears above her, a tall glass of ice water in hand. She takes it and quickly drinks down half. It's cool, fresh, and exactly what she needs. Delightful to her senses. She focuses fully on Henri as he sits beside her looking delectable in every way.

"I'm sorry, *cher*, I didn't think…"

"I'm fine. It just took me off guard. Again." She chuckles at her own expense and sips her water. "I should've known better after the last time."

He smiles and shakes his head. "You'd already been drinking. I should've known."

"Stop. It's fine. I'm fine." She places the cup on the table and lies back. "In fact, I actually really like it. I feel pretty good. Everything feels good." She giggles and levels her gaze on him, drinking in the handsome line of his jaw and the way his brow comes together the tiniest bit as he looks her over with concern. "I bet *you* feel good," she purrs, reaching out her hand to him. He takes it in his and kisses her knuckles, sending thrills run up her arm as his breath tickles her skin. "Mmm, you do," she whispers, closing her eyes to fall completely into the sensation. "I knew you would." Her words are a mere breath. "Can I feel more of you?" she asks, surprising herself with her boldness.

It isn't the alcohol talking. Sure, she'd been tipsy when she took that hit, but now she is a new kind of inebriated. Not stumbling about or seeing double. No. Her mind is clear, her senses sharp. She knows exactly what she wants. Henri's touch. She wants his kiss. She wants to feel his skin against hers with this heightened awareness. If his lips on her fingers felt like this, what would they feel like all over her body?

"Let's go upstairs," she says softly.

"You sure?" Henri asks, still holding her hand to his lips, looking up, his expression full of desire.

"I'm sure." She stands, her head and body feel light. She's floating in her space. His hand over hers is a welcome anchor.

Climbing the stairs for the second time that night, Bridgette is in a different headspace. Where dread and anxiety had coiled themselves in her chest before, she's now bursting with anticipation. The storm still rages outside, but inside it's warm and safe. All the what-ifs and whys have drifted away, replaced by the possibilities of why not. She realizes at the top of the stairs how fully in the moment she is. A rare experience for her.

She turns to see Henri two steps down wearing a decadent grin. "You sure you're all right?" he asks, stopping and placing one hand against the wall.

"I'm sure that I'm sure." She smiles. Golden light from his bedroom spills onto the floor. His eyes shine with it.

He hurries up the last two steps and wraps her in his arms. The thrill is instant. His touch is the only thing she knows. With his lips on hers she's utterly lost. They sway together to the music of the rain and wind. He sighs and pulls away. A few swipes on his phone and a beautiful female voice singing in French over a soft and sensual beat fills the air.

Bridgette closes her eyes and rocks to and fro. Then Henri's leading her through the door.

They're dancing in place. His eyes dazzling, her heart full to bursting. With one hand on her cheek he moves in for another sweet and searching kiss. His lips so tender against hers. The warmth starts as an ember then burns through her to the tips of her fingers and toes. Her body is alight with the sensation. It radiates from his touch on her cheek, his kiss, and his hand on the small of her back.

As they dance, Bridgette urges them toward the bed, one small step at a time. Nearing it, she pulls out of his embrace to slip her shirt over her head. Henri does the same. He's against her again, crushing her to his chest.

She snakes her arms around him and presses her cheek to his heart, relishing his smooth warmth. His swollen cock nudges her belly. She slips her arms free and lowers herself to her knees, tugging his pants down. The natural musk from his dark, curling hairs mingles with his perfumed scent. She sighs and looks up, licking her lips and reaching for his rigid shaft.

His hands are on hers quickly. He pulls her up to her feet then lifts her by her waist, easily onto the bed. He pulls off her pants, kicks out of his own, and steps between her legs. Resting his hands on her thighs, he looks her over.

She smiles and scoots closer to him. His hands slide up, his thumbs nestle in the crease where hip meet thigh. He gives a light squeeze and her core quivers. She can feel the heat from his cock so near her pulsing lips. With one hand he pushes his swollen head against her clit. A tiny eruption strikes and she breathes in quickly, shocked by her sensitivity.

Every point of contact is blooming with pleasure. His cock against her clit, his hand kneading her hip, his legs against her thighs. Then his lips are on hers again. She's lost, scooting closer, aching to have him. She rolls her hips, urging him on. He answers with only the tip, circling it barely inside her. She tries to move closer, to take him fully. But he's pinned her to the bed with his one hand on her hip.

She's suspended in desire, yearning for more, yet thrilled beyond measure. She falls back in surrender, her body tingling with arousal, her cheeks burning.

Henri continues working his magic, easing in a bit at a time, exploring her fully, exposing points of pleasure she didn't know she had. As he finds them, she grinds against him, panting and quaking until he moves on. His knuckles press into her labia as he measures his strokes. The ecstasy that follows is beyond comprehension. It ripples from her core, spreading throughout her body. A moan escapes her mouth. A song without words. A song of bliss. Somewhere in that song, he gathers her to him. He's holding her close, her legs wrapped tightly around him. He's deep inside her, thrusting. She wraps her arms around him, burying her face in his chest, unsure of where he stops and she begins.

Then, she's lying on a pile of pillows, sure she won't come back. She'll die there and be happy for it. He's above her, silken smooth and smiling as he rocks deep inside her, touching places no one has. Her arms are weak, her legs jelly. She sighs, attempting speech. He breathes in her ear, a soothing sound, more tingling joy. Then his body goes taut and he's pulsing. Another ripple of delight. His lips on her face. Her heavy eyes close. A soft blanket covers her cold skin.

"Mmm," she hums. She blinks slowly, looking over Henri's glowing face. "You sure know how to help a lady relax." She yawns, manages a smile, then sleep welcomes her.

***

Henri dozes beside Bridgette, his heart full with terrifying and wonderful emotions. Her weight beside him is a strange yet welcome thing. Lightning glimmers and thunder sounds, low and rumbling in the distance. The rain falls peacefully off the balcony, the sound causing his heavy eyelids to succumb to exhaustion.

Somewhere out of the cottony darkness drifts the sound of wheels on a half-pipe. A strobe light flashes. Fluorescent graffiti shines intense and otherworldly. Bodies everywhere, crowd around him in a smoky haze. Henri brushes away one cloud to find himself in another. They cling like cobwebs. The wheels roll and clack somewhere in the distance. With every flash of light, he sees more faces from his past. His parents, his siblings, his friends. They pantomime scenes from his life. Random, meaningless moments. The smoke closes in, blinding him. He follows the sound of the half-pipe. Searching for one face.

Laughter, sad and haunting. So much smoke. Then Dottie is at the top of the half-pipe, board in her hand, cigarette hanging from her bottom lip. She takes one long drag, inhaling all the smoke into her lungs. The warehouse is empty. Henri and Dottie stand alone in the flickering lights.

"Let's get out of here," she says, flicking her cigarette away, taking a pull from her whiskey bottle.

They're driving too fast. She's driving too fast. "You said you would go with me. You said we'd go together," she screams. Her eyes are wild and drunk, and she's crying.

"Dot, I didn't mean now. Not so soon. You had to know. How could I leave now?"

"You're right. Why would you leave? You have everything you could ever want." Her words are like venom, a shock to his young and foolish heart. Her eyes flash with rage as she looks away from the road to him. Headlights glare, horns blast.

Then he's upside down, hanging from his seatbelt. Glass everywhere, glittering with blood. Dottie's gone, her body a twisted lump in the distance. He struggles to escape, crawls through broken glass and gravel to her side. Her face is broken, full of blood and glass. Her eyes stare cold and dead to the heavens. Henri chokes on his tears and screams a silent scream.

He wakes, soaked in sweat and panting. The image of Dottie's face, cracked and bleeding, doesn't fade. Bridgette shifts beside him then settles, undisturbed. He rises slowly, careful not to wake her, and leaves the room, knowing all too well that sleep won't come again this night.

It's been so long since he dreamed of that night. Countless hours of therapy had done what years of self-medicating and denial couldn't. Fretfully, he wonders why tonight of all nights he would dream that dream again. The memories of the aftermath crowd for attention in his weary mind. First the sirens, then the hospital. His mom's face pale and distant. His dad's red with anger. Their words lost to painkillers and shock. Henri had asked for Dot repeatedly. They shook their heads. The police came. His dad sent them away.

The next day, before his bruises had time to heal, he was on a plane to Japan. Pushed away by his family. The only comfort he'd been offered was a substantial monthly allowance. They'd told him he would stay in Japan until things blew over. "A year at the most." One year became many. He'd been forgotten. He grew to adulthood with no guidance, exploring the world as only a wealthy pseudo-orphan could. It wasn't until his oldest brother's wedding that he was invited back. Even then, he was held at a distance. No one mentioned why he left. No one spoke of Dottie or her family as if they never existed.

He holds his head in his hands, the pain too great to bear. His throat grows tight as tears well in his eyes. Who would she be today? A formidable woman for sure. He thinks of Lilian, her gruff and husky voice, her no-bullshit persona. He recalls all the women who sat around the table at the bar with Bridgette. Dottie could easily be one of them. But no. She never had the chance to discover the beautifully shameless world of burlesque. Never had a chance to discover the woman she was meant to be. All because he made promises he couldn't keep. His love had been selfish and she had paid the ultimate price. Now, with a precious woman in his bed, is he about to make the same mistake?

***

Henri stands in the doorway watching Bridgette sleep. Her tousled silken hair is spread out on the pillows around her. His heart is so full it's as though it could crawl up out of his chest and into his hands so he could give it to her. As he stands in the darkened room, the light from the hallway casts gently on her peaceful face, if she would wake with sleepy eyes and her generous smile and accept his offering.

He considers sliding back into bed beside her and holding her until his pain eases. He can kiss her face and touch her skin until he forgets about the dream, about his past. If he can push it away for two more days, she'll never have to know, and he'll never have to see on her beautiful face the heartache and judgment that will surely be there. She can go back to Chicago unaware of what he had done. And, sadly, he'll go back to business as usual. Casual relationships with casual women who gladly accept his gifts in place of real connection. Women who don't care to know who he is or why. Women who don't challenge his existence with their bold honesty and unapologetic truths.

But he can't. She deserves better than that. As Dottie had. So he watches for a bit more, committing Bridgette's face to memory, taking as much warmth and joy as he can from the moment. Then he dresses and heads downstairs. He writes a quick note and walks out into the rain.

Chapter 15

Bridgette wakes to Bones licking her face. He whines and jumps off the bed, running in quick circles between her and the door. She rubs the sleep from her eyes and sits up. The floor is cold under her feet. Henri's nowhere to be seen. His side of the bed is barely rumpled.

"All right, all right. I'm coming," she tells the dog as she slides from the bed, gathering her clothes from the floor. Outside it's gray and wet. Though the storm seems to've passed, the rain continues to fall in steady, heavy sheets. "Come on, boy. I bet he went for coffee." She yawns and follows Bones out of the room and down the stairs. Opening the door, as she had seen Henri do a few times the night before, she watches Bones hurry into the rain. On the table by the door is a note written in Henri's fine scrawl.

> *Ma Cher,*
> *So sorry, something came up. I didn't want to wake*
> *you. Not sure how long I'll be. Make yourself at*
> *home. Apologies for Bones, he's a bit spoiled and*
> *loves attention.*
> *– Henri*

"Hm," she hums to the empty foyer then opens the door to look for Bones. He's sitting on the porch, tail wagging. He stands and shakes the rain from his coat, misting her bare arms and feet, then runs past her into the kitchen. She follows. His food and water dishes are empty, and she goes to the cabinet where Henri keeps Bones's food. She fills the bowls and he dives in hungrily. "Did Henri forget to feed you?" she asks, searching the kitchen for coffee and a pot. The house feels too quiet without Henri. Quiet and much bigger. She puts on the coffee and goes to find her phone.

In Henri's bedroom, she watches the rain through the window and wishes he were there with her. She pouts at the empty bed, realizing how much she wants to snuggle into the pillows and blankets with him. Her phone buzzes inside her purse, which is on top of her other bags. She takes it out and climbs back under the covers, hoping the message is from Henri and he's on his way home from wherever he went. Her shoulders slump. It's Lilian. Not interested in "thanks for visiting" pleasantries, Bridgette leaves the message unanswered and snuggles down into the bed. If she can get back to sleep, Henri can wake her when he gets home. Then they can have the sexy, sleepy morning this rainy day was made for.

With her eyes closed, she listens to the gentle shower outside, the heaviness of sleep is beyond her reach. She dreams of Henri's arrival and making love in one alluring position after another. She revels in the softness of his bedding and his scent all around her. Time moves slowly. The smell of coffee drifts up from the kitchen. Bones wanders in, sniffs her bare foot, and leaves uninterested. She sighs and wonders where Henri went, staring at the bright white ceiling. Her phone pings again. She reaches for it quickly. It's Lilian.

This guy look familiar?

Attached is a screenshot of an old article from *The Times-Picayune*. The headline reads "Son of Prominent New Orleans Family Only Survivor in Deadly Crash." Beneath it is a black and white picture of the wreckage. Next to that is Henri's smiling face, in what looks like a yearbook picture. He was a kid, but she'd recognize his smile anywhere. Bridgette's heart drops to her stomach. Tears touch the corners of her eyes.

How about this one?

Another screen shot of a newspaper. It's young Henri walking out of the hospital, his face bandaged, his eyes vacant. His mom trying her best to not be seen. His dad holding him by the back of the arm. The headline reads "Minor, Henry Dauphine Headed to Trial for Manslaughter." Bridgette's face goes numb. Her stomach churns and rolls. She's heartbroken, and furious, and scared. She stares at the haunting image of Henri and his parents. His words play over in her mind. "…getting into a lot of trouble… had no control over me… a family matter…"

"Fuck." Her expletive breaks the peaceful quiet of the room as she dials Lilian's number.

"Hey," Lilian answers with a whisper.

"Hey. What the fuck. How'd did you find these?"

"I'm at the library looking up old films."

"Why?"

"Trixie remembered something about homeboy's disappearance while we were smoking last night. She didn't have a lot of details, but I figured I'd check it out for you. What a fella, huh?"

"Yeah…" Bridgette swallows hard, looking at herself tucked neatly into his bed. "How did she forget a thing like this?"

"Trixie'll remember what you wore to lunch three years ago and every word you spoke at said lunch, but she'll forget it was her birthday. She's got her own way of cataloging things. I'm glad something jarred her memory. I knew I didn't like him."

"But I mean, it's not like he did it on purpose." Silence on the other end of the phone. Bridgette's stomach hurts terribly, and her mouth is dry.

"No, but the way he hid it. The way they covered it up," Lilian says quickly. "Fucking bourgeoisie. What time you fly out today?"

"I'm not leaving today."

"What?" she asks, no longer attempting a whisper. "Why not?"

"Mike was afraid we'd get stuck in the airport because of the storm. We decided to stay until Wednesday."

"Cool. Cool. We should get together again before you go. There's so much more to this story."

"Yeah there is."

"Huh?"

"Well, um. I'm in his house right now waiting for him to come home."

"What?" Lilian's voice rises well above a library-appropriate volume. "What are you doing there?"

"I spent the night with him. Spent the last two nights with him, actually."

"Shit, baby. I didn't realize it was like that. Kinda thought I was only spreading some gossip around."

"Yeah, no. It's like that, I guess. It's definitely like something." She looks around Henri's room. It's beautifully decorated with fine furniture and antique fixtures. The light gray walls are adorned with expertly chosen artwork. But there's no sign of the person who sleeps here, no character. The dresser and side tables are empty save for the lamps. It's not a bedroom, it's a showroom. The whole house is a showroom. The more she thinks about it the less she likes it.

"You still there?" Lilian asks.

"Yeah. But I'm gonna let you go. I've got to wrap my head around this."

"Yeah, okay. Stay safe."

"You too. Thanks." Bridgette drops her phone on the bed beside her. Her mind is buzzing, struggling to form complete thoughts. Her heart aches. The word manslaughter runs on repeat along with Lilian's words. *...there's so much more to this story.* Bridgette has to get up, get dressed, and get out of there.

Bones yips downstairs as the door opens. Henri's doggie greeting floats up the stairs.

***

After he leaves, he walks aimlessly through the rainy streets, umbrella in hand. His feet take him miles away from his home and Bridgette. He finds himself standing under a sprawling oak in Holt Cemetery surrounded by low and broken shadows of derelict headstones. Most are tilted and sunken. Some are made of splintered wood or PVC pipe. The black sky has faded, puddles glisten in the streetlamps and turn to rippling white pools reflecting the morning sky. Through the rain, he looks over the moldering headstones to the one he is there to see.

Dottie Evelynn Pearl
1979–1996
Gone too soon

He remembers the first time he visited after years of mourning her from the other side of the globe. He'd been shocked to find her final resting place forgotten and unkempt. It seemed her family had buried her and never looked back. Knowing of the substantial settlement the Dauphines paid the Pearls, he couldn't believe they hadn't given her a better burial.

Henri spent years doing his penance, visiting weekly to tend her grave with his own hands. He'd placed the small black fence around it, planted flowers, and pulled weeds. But, eventually, his weekly visits turned to every other week, then once a month. Monthly visits fell to random stops when his guilt weighed heavily. Then once a year on the anniversary of her death. Until the day came that he realized he missed it altogether. As he stands with sore legs and tight shoulders, he notices how little has changed since the last time he left a garish bouquet to wilt against her headstone.

"I'm sorry, Dottie." His voice cracks as he kneels in a muddy puddle, dropping his umbrella. Rain and tears run down his face. "I don't know what to do." He chokes on his swollen throat. "Not a day goes by I don't think of you. That I don't regret every wrong I ever did." He swipes at his face and drops on one hip, slouching and sobbing. "How do I move on?"

She doesn't answer. "I thought I was doing so well." He sits with his knees up to rest his elbows on them. The only sound is the rain pattering all around. "They say it wasn't my fault. But I know I could've done more. I could've helped you be happier here. I could've kept you safe." He sighs, swiping at his wet face and sopping hair. "They say that it wasn't my responsibility... I was just a kid."

He turns his face skyward, letting the raindrops wash his tears away. "They say you were sick in the head. But I know you weren't sick. You were miserable. You wanted a way out. And I promised you one. I promised you and I failed you."

The hiss of a car's tires spraying water as it passes nearby seems appropriate. He drops his face down, rain running over his neck. "I can't keep going like this. I've wished so many times that I died that night with you. But what would it matter? I'd be tucked up in some tomb miles away and you'd still be here, rotting in that same dirt box." He sighs, thoroughly soaked and defeated.

"I don't know what to do," he says softly, the pain as raw as it had been in those first helpless days. "I'm so sorry." He sits silent in the company of cracked and decrepit headstones, watching the rain splash in the murky puddle between his feet. His once-white sneakers are caked with mud and dirt.

"Hey, you okay?" a gruff voice asks from above him. He looks up to see an older man in coveralls and a baseball cap. He's standing with his hands in his pockets and a concerned frown. "You all right, man?"

"Yeah," Henri answers, moving to stand. The stranger steps forward to offer assistance. Henri waves him back.

"Is it early or late for ya?" the man asks, stepping back, eyeing Henri curiously. "Looks like it's a late one."

Henri wipes his hands on his sopping pants and brushes his heavy hair from his face. "It is," he answers, embarrassed. The stranger bites his cheek and nods once with understanding.

"You need a ride? I'm heading downtown."

Henri stares and realizes how far from home he is. His tortured walk had taken hours as he wandered through the rainy night. He clears his throat and straightens himself. "I would appreciate it." He nods, wiping at the rain on his face again.

"All right then, let's go." He turns and starts walking. Henri follows. "Don't worry 'bout the mud. You can't hurt this upholstery," the man says over his shoulder as they approach a pickup older than Henri and every bit as rough. He climbs into the passenger side. The cab smells of cheap cigars and old coffee. The springs of the bench seat are visible in several places. His chauffeur gets in and turns the key, and the engine rumbles and roars to life. "Where ya goin?" They pull away from the curb, while the old wiper blades squeak loud and fast. Henri looks at the man, his face a mass of deeply furrowed wrinkles and sparse gray whiskers.

"Magazine," Henri answers more smoothly than he expected. He clears his throat. "Thank you for this. I'm not sure what my plans were for getting home."

"Meh. It's nothing. I saw you out there. Looked like you could use a hand." They ride the rest of the way in silence. Henri looks out the window, his mind, body, and soul frayed. He is exhausted and wet. His thoughts prevent any semblance of peace.

"I'm not going to ask you what you were doing there last night. Seems pretty obvious to me," the man says out of nowhere. Henri looks from his window to the man. His eyes are fixed on the road. He behaves as if he'd said nothing, and smacks his thick droopy lips. Henri settles in for more silence, watching the city through the windows.

Henri surveys his muddy clothes and dirt-streaked hands and thinks of Bridgette sleeping so peacefully in his bed. In his chest is a battle between the newfound joy he feels with her and the ever-present grief and frustration that has thumped its rhythm in his pulse for years.

"You gotta leave the dead where they lay, boy," the old man says, fishing a small thin cigar out of its pack with his lips, his eyes on the road. With one hand on the wheel, he lights it. The cab fills with sweet and noxious smoke. "There's too much livin' to do out here." He blows out a raspy cloud of smoke.

"Easier said than done." Henri sighs, pushing his wet hair out of his eyes.

"Maybe. But don't think for a second the dead lose any sleep over you. Death ain't hard for the dead. Death only hurts the living." The man takes a long drag from his cigar and minds the road. Henri watches him with curiosity as the truck shakes and bounces over the broken city streets. "Whereabouts on Magazine?" the old guy asks, ashing the cigar on the floor. The smoke in the cab is overwhelming. Henri's lungs scream for freedom.

"Anywhere will do." He gestures without commitment. "I appreciate getting as far as I have. It *was* a long night," he says, looking forward to a shower and clean air. The truck turns onto Magazine and slows to a stop. Henri opens the door, grateful for the fresh air, no matter how wet. "Thank you for the ride," he says, turning to smile at his new friend. The old man looks at him, his brows furrowed.

"You've got plenty of time to spend sulking around a graveyard once you're dead." He waves his cigar in Henri's direction. "Don't waste your time doin' it now." He pops the cigar back between his teeth and gives Henri a quick nod. Henri nods back and closes the door. The truck rambles away without a pause.

Henri stands in the rain, thankful to be so close to home and Bridgette.

Chapter 16

Bridgette swallows hard, not ready to see Henri. She stands in his room, feet heavy on the floor, head full of questions. If only she'd had more time to process the information, to prepare. His voice travels up the stairs. She steps toward the door, wondering if she should tell him she knows about what happened while fighting the urge to lock herself in the bathroom again.

He's still the same person, she tells herself, stepping closer to the door. *But who is that, really?* Her old friend fear begins to whisper its warnings in her mind. *Who is he?* The constant buzz of dread creeps up the back of her neck, resting in the base of her skull. *You should get out of here.* Her heart is in her throat, thumping wildly. The rational part of her brain weighs in. *He's Henri. You don't know him well, but you know him.* She reaches the door and swallows hard, forcing her heartbeat to slow.

"Good morning," she calls in the brightest voice she can muster. She stands at the top of the stairs looking down. Her false smile disappears the moment she sees him. Instead of his playful grin and perfectly placed hair, she's greeted by haunted eyes and matted locks. The longer she stares the more terrible the picture becomes. He's soaked and covered in mud, his shoulders slumped, his face pinched. A weak smile lifts the corners of his lips as his gaze meets hers.

"Hey," he calls and continues to stare with large, glistening eyes. "Sorry I took off. I…" His words trail away as he looks from her down to his filthy pants. He makes a little sound and kicks out of his shoes, a puddle forming where he stands. Bones wags his tail and runs circles around him. "It's all right, boy." He bends to pat the dog's head. "I need a shower, that's all." He stands straight and steps toward the stairs. Bridgette's heart races. She steps back into his room as he ascends the stairs. He looks like he's just buried a body.

"What happened?" she asks as he enters the room, little more than a ghost of the sexy, confident man she'd made love with for the past two nights.

He sighs and his shoulders drop, even lower. "It's complicated." He passes her and is heading into the bathroom. He leaves the door open and peels away the wet and muddy clothes. "I'm sorry, *cher.*" He sounds defeated. "I'm not used to having guests." She hears the shower go on.

"Maybe I should go," she calls over the running water. Her cheeks burn, and her mouth is dry. Looking at her bags stacked neatly beside the bed, she remembers her dress on the bathroom floor. On tiptoes she sneaks in. Henri's back is to her behind the glass door of the shower, one hand against the wall as he lets the water run over the back of his head. She stands, holding her damp dress, watching him through the fogging glass. Despite his browbeaten posture, his lean muscled shoulders are strong and sure. Though broken and sad, he radiates beauty and kindness, which is all she's ever known from him.

She remembers Bunny's observation about her liking his energy and for the moment chooses to forget Henri's secrets and odd behavior. She pushes her fear deep down and steps closer to the glass. Henri looks up. Their gazes meet. The pain she sees in the lines of his face pulls at her heart. He begs without words for acceptance, for kindness, for love. She sees her own fear and pain reflected in his tortured eyes. She sees him without his mask, raw and vulnerable.

"Don't go," he says softly, his lips barely moving.

She strips bare in an instant and slips in beside him. Warm spray from the water hits her dry cold skin. Her heart is thumping, but the need to be near him is beyond fear and desire. His torment aches deep in her chest.

He turns to face her, the warm water streaming down his face and chest. His normally smiling lips hang slack with despair. Reaching out gingerly, she touches his face. He closes his bloodshot eyes and leans into her touch. Then, with both arms, he pulls her close, crushing her to him. The warm water rushes over her as his hot, slippery skin meets hers. He holds her with urgency, pressing his cheek to the top of her head.

Her body arches into his as she winds her arms around his back. He sobs silently against her and lowers himself to his knees. His face presses against her belly as his body shakes with grief-filled spasms. The warm water hits her face and chest as she holds his head in her hands, wondering what happened. What brought this confident, playful man to his knees, crying in a puddle at her feet?

"Hey," she says gently after he goes still. "Let's get out of here."

***

Henri's damp and heavy head lies sleeping on her chest. Bridgette sits propped against a mountain of pillows, processing. Once they were dry and comfortable in his bed, he spoke without tears. His words spilled like a river from a broken damn. He told her everything there was to tell about Dottie Pearl.

He spoke first of meeting her and falling madly in love. Of giving his teenage heart to her in an instant. He talked about her life and her family, and how unhappy she'd been. How they promised to run away together. Then, through choked words he revisited the fateful night where, in his mind, he failed her. The night she died and he survived.

Though clearly ragged and worn, he went on. He painted a different picture of his years abroad than he had the night before. He talked of loneliness and heartbreak, of longing for a family that rejected him. He shared instances from years of drugs and alcohol to ease the pain, which he finally left behind when he went into therapy. Then he told her of his late night wandering the streets only to find himself at the cemetery, and how he ended up soaking wet and covered in mud.

Bridgette had listened patiently, without judgment. She fought her tears, feeling his pain as real and visceral as if it were her own. Then, when it seemed he was done, she opened her arms, welcoming him into her embrace. She held him in silence as he relaxed and drifted to sleep.

After everything he told her, she feels angry and hurt *for him*. He'd been abandoned when he needed love the most. His family sent him away to save themselves. They sent him away a child, scared and heartbroken, to face the world on his own. To process his grief and self-loathing without support. She couldn't believe a mother could be so callous.

Then she remembers her own mother. Bridgette's countless nights alone wondering when her mother would be home. All the weekends and holidays she spent with her grandparents while her mom tried to "make it work" again. She remembers her father showing up with gifts and promises he had no intention of keeping. At least Bridgette had had her grandma and grandpa. They were always a phone call away, despite the constant feeling that she was their greatest burden. Henri had been truly alone. A teenager left to navigate the most difficult time of his life in a strange world with family he'd never met.

She considers his struggles and her own. So different, yet somehow the same, both forced to grow up and face the world far too soon by uncaring parents. Stroking his bare shoulder absently and gazing at his sleeping profile, she's overwhelmed with a feeling so full it's frightening. She imagines who he would be had he not experienced such tragedy so young. What would he have done with the opportunities he surely lost? College? An upstanding profession like his brothers? A family of his own?

She wipes at the tears in the corners of her eyes and slides out from his sleeping embrace.

***

Henri wakes to a gray sky and an empty bed. He feels ragged yet refreshed. And though his embarrassment weighs heavy, it's nothing to the years of grief he's been carrying. He lies in shock, remembering how much of himself he revealed. Then he recalls the way she welcomed his tears with understanding eyes and open arms. She'd held him without judgment and met him in a place where he'd always been alone.

He had known there was something special about her the moment he saw her. Has it really only been four days since she disappeared from that voodoo shop a beautiful, mysterious stranger? It seems, somehow, she's always been there in his bed and his heart. But no. Her stack of luggage is proof, if he needed it. Not only has she been there for a short time, their time together is coming to an end. Henri moves out of the bed and hurries down the stairs to find her.

She's sitting, feet tucked beneath her on the couch, a plate of cheese and meats balanced on her lap, her phone in her hand. Bones looks up from the other end of the couch, his tail wagging as Henri walks in. Bridgette looks up and smiles brightly.

"Hey," he says sheepishly, standing in the doorway.

"How are you feeling?" she asks gently, shifting to make room for him.

"I'm good." He sits. "Really good, actually."

"I'm glad." She places her plate on the table and settles back into the couch.

They sit in silence. Henri looks at his hands in his lap, unsure of what to say. Unsure of how to move forward. What's there to say after you've revealed so much of yourself?

"I found out we're flying out first thing Wednesday morning." Henri's heart sinks at the thought. She's brought such a beautiful light to his otherwise dark life, the idea of that light going out after only a few days is unbearable.

"You sure you want to do that?" He hopes it comes across as a playful question and doesn't sound as desperate as it feels.

"What do you mean?" She laughs. "Of course I want to go home."

Ouch. Well, what did you expect? You just showed her what a waste of space you are. Why would she want to stay with you?

"I wish I could stay for a while longer. But real life is calling." She reaches for her plate and starts munching again.

"You should ignore the call." He shifts in his seat, turning in her direction. "Stay for as long as you'd like. I could hire you."

"To do what?" She scrunches her nose.

"Well, I only recently got Jo in the studio to record. If he likes what he hears, we'll need album art. I'd like to set him up with an entire brand. But you'd have to be here to do photos and whatnot…" She eyes him skeptically, his offer hanging in the air.

"I can't," she says with a small shake of her head. "It's an intriguing offer, for sure., but I don't have any of my equipment here, not even my laptop."

"You could get those things. Right?"

"They're in Chicago," she says slowly. "Nine hundred miles away."

"What I meant was you could get them and come back. I'll pay for your flight."

"I'll stay here?"

"Well, I thought so. But if you'd rather…" He's stumbling over his words. "I mean, I could get you a suite if you'd like, anywhere you want to stay."

"It's tempting." She places her napkin on the table. "But I've got so many projects in the works. It's bad enough that I've been away from them this long. In fact, now I'm stressing over them." She gives a small laugh. "Like I really should've brought my laptop."

"How about when you're finished with those projects? Can I book you then?"

She narrows her eyes at him. "You'd have to make it worth my time."

Henri's heart soars. She could name her price and he'd pay it. Any amount. He'd double it. "Now that's something I can do."

"Okay. Cool. I've got at least three weeks' worth of work before I'm free and clear. Then we've got a show coming up. I can't miss that. I'm looking at a month before I can make it back. Would that work?" she asks, her tone all business.

Henri smiles. "Yeah, whatever works for you." He's already looking forward to her return. "Would you like to listen to his album?" He's becoming excited about the potential of the project. With Jo's sound and Bridgette's eye for photography and design, they could create something magical.

Chapter 17

Jo's music *is* New Orleans. It's aching and ragged, then spiraling with joy, down home yet complicated and intricate. That's the instrumentals. Once Jo's low, gravelly baritone joins in, the sound is an instrument in and of itself, and his lyrics pull at Bridgette's heart. He sings of devastation and hope, love and rage, joy and grief. Every song is a beautiful glimpse into his soul.

"He's amazing," Bridgette says. They're sitting side by side in his sound room. He's on his rolling leather office chair. She's on a soft bench they pulled in from the hallway. "Like, he's legitimately magic or something." She's brushing a tear from the corner of her eye.

The feelings that welled in her chest as she listened to the most recent song were overwhelming. The lyrics were already lost in the air, as new songs were wont to do. But loss and acceptance lingered as the last note from the guitar faded.

"I told you he was amazing." Henri grins and shakes his head. "He's never been recorded."

"Really?"

"Really. He's always been against it. Thought it would take something away from the sound. I bet he hasn't even listened to the demo I gave him."

"I understand what he means. I hate watching videos of my performances. There is something so special about being live in front of an audience. Now I wish I'd paid closer attention to him on Friday night. But...I was a bit distracted." She tilts her chin down to watch Henri scroll through the song list, his eyes on the computer screen, one foot tapping an absent beat.

"Were you?" he asks with an eyebrow raised, eyes still on the screen.

"Were *you*?" she teases. He looks to her with smiling eyes, but a serious expression.

"I've been distracted since early Friday afternoon." A small smile plays at the corners of his mouth. Bridgette scans his face. His smooth brow. The fine line of his jaw. The shadow of stubble on his chin that looks delectable to touch and would feel rough against her skin.

"Me too," she says, holding his gaze, willing him to make the first move.

"You're going to love this next one," he says with a bright smile as he turns his attention back to the computer. She'd be disappointed if he wasn't so adorable in his zeal. With one click, the music starts. A single drumbeat, then Jo's voice.

You'll be my psychotherapy...

The drum plays its slow, steady beat.

You'll be my guru too...

The drum is joined by a haunting blues guitar.

'Cause it's written on our scars and on every inch of you.
We started something the moment that we touched
We started something didn't think I'd
Like it this much
We started something the moment that we kissed
We started something didn't know it could
Feel like this

The drums and guitar are joined by some brass, low and sexy. Jo's voice blends perfectly with the sound, beginning the second verse.

You'll be my arch-nemesis
My sinner, my saint
'Cause you're everything I've ever been
And everything I ain't
We started something the moment that we touched
We started something didn't think I'd
Like it this much
We started something the moment that we kissed
We started something didn't know it could
Feel like this

The music plays on, building to a guitar solo. Then, slowing for the next verse.

You'll be my angel, my devil
My savior, my demise

Every dream I've ever had
Is in your lips and in your eyes
We started something the moment that we touched
We started something didn't think I'd
Like it this much
We started something the moment that we kissed
We started something didn't know it could
Feel like this

The brass fades, then the guitar. The single drumbeat plays out.

You'll be my psychotherapy
You'll be my guru too…

"Wow," Bridgette gushes.

Henri looks at her, grinning. "Right?"

"Yeah. He's brilliant. Does he write all of his lyrics?"

"He writes everything."

"Of course he does. You're right. I love that song. I would love to make a video for it. I've got a dozen ideas already." Henri's gaze is intense on her. He's turned completely in his chair, his hand no longer on the mouse.

"I believe it. I'd love to see what you come up with."

"I'd love to show you." Bridgette's tone is soft, sultry. She's done talking about music.

"Show me now." He replays the song. Its slow, sexy drum beat cuts the silence. Suddenly, she's bashful. Her cheeks warm with the idea of what he's requesting.

"Really?" She gestures to her baggy shirt and sweatpants. Then the messy bun bobbing on the top of her head.

"Yeah, really."

She stares at him as the song plays. Its rhythm begs to be danced to. Under her awkward blush, her body longs to answer that call. Though she's danced in sweats more times than she can count at practice, this doesn't feel right. Dancing in heels and glitter doesn't seem right either. As they sit, listening to the song, their gazes fixed on each other, Henri silently goads her on. The drum beat pulls at her hips. She sighs heavily, giving in to her hips and his yearning.

"Give me two minutes," she says as she stands. "Stay put." She crosses the hall to his bedroom.

***

Henri waits patiently for her return. Two minutes becomes ten, then twenty. The song is playing on a loop. Bridgette appears in the doorway as it begins again, draped in the silk scarf he bought her and nothing else. Her hair is down, smooth and somehow wild. Her face is makeup free; only the blush of her excitement colors her cheeks. She seems timid, almost hesitant, then Jo starts singing.

She slinks into the room with grace and confidence, sidestepping the bench and moving around his back. The scarf dances around her curves. She stands behind him, wrapping her arms around his shoulders. She kisses his ear lightly and spins his seat to face the open space in the room and she steps back into it. She arches and spins to the music, her body part of the melody. The silk scarf slides off her shoulder, revealing the smallest glimpse of skin. Her nipples sharp and pointed as it glides over them. Then she turns, her back to him. The scarf dips down to her ass, a peek of one cheek, then the other. A half turn, he sees her profile. The silken fabric gathers around her, bunched at her hip. Her shapely thigh, her smooth shoulder exposed. Her hair hiding half of her face.

The smirk on her sweet, dainty mouth drives him to a point of madness. She steps toward him then mounts the bench, still wrapped in silk. He pushes his chair away to get the full view of her riding the bench. She grinds and twists, still holding the scarf in place, never revealing more than a taste of skin. Then she brings her legs up and lies back, resplendent on the bench, pointing one toe then the other. Her hair spreads around her, hanging off the bench. Her face serene, eyes closed, mouth sensual and smiling. The scarf covering her pert breasts and soft stomach. It slips away from her thighs, revealing the cleft of her mound.

The sight of her spread out, lost in her own ecstasy, is too much. The gentleman in him is gone, and he moves from his chair without pause.

He's over her in an instant. Her eyes flash open, surprised at first, then pleased. She smiles slowly and licks her lips. He's on his knees beside her, feeling her warm skin under the smooth silk. As he's exploring every delectable curve, her breath catches in her throat. His lips are on hers, and she tastes delicious.

Her hands come up to his face, holding it while she kisses back hungrily. He moves his mouth over her chin, then down her neck, kissing through the silk. His breath is hot in the delicate weave of the fabric. She purrs as he moves over her body, kissing and biting down to her exposed cleft.

He breathes in her scent, then dips his tongue along her sensitive skin, tasting her sweet saltiness. She squirms, and her legs fall open. She's wet and swollen, her thighs damp. He laps at her, relishing her taste, nipping her skin with his lips and teeth.

The scarf falls from her body, and her bare skin seems to scream for attention. His hands move over her, cupping and squeezing her breasts, tweaking her nipples. He moves to take them in his mouth, one then the other, rolling his tongue over their swollen points.

Her fingers are in his hair, gripping at the root. They move down his neck. Tingles run down his back and over his scalp. She pulls at his shirt and removes it, then she sits up, straddling the bench. Her expression says it all.

He drops his pants and joins her on the bench. His cock solid, standing at attention.

She takes him in her hand and starts stroking. He shudders, pleasure coursing through him. She inches closer. Her lips are on his, and she licks at them as she strokes his shaft. Then she rises only to lower herself onto him. He's buried deep in her slippery, satin folds.

She moans as she grinds, her legs over his, wrapped around his waist. The bench creaks under their weight. He shifts to push her onto her back. She rolls her hips, her breasts rippling with each rotation. Henri watches her writhing with pleasure, his dick pulsing in response. His hands run the length of her torso, over her rib cage to her breasts, then back to her hips. Her arms hang down. She grips the legs of the bench. She continues to roll and grind into him, her eyes closed, her mouth open, panting her breaths.

He untangles himself from her legs and stands above her. She looks up, her brow knit, her bottom lip pouting. Without words she pleads for more. He tugs at her hip gently. She responds by rising up on her knees, balancing on the bench. He moves behind her. She lowers her face to the cushion, her ass raised in the air, wiggling, waiting.

His cock twitches as he admires her full, round cheeks and swollen lips on display. He plunges in, deep and wild. His hands squeeze her hips then caress the soft, shaking globes. She cries into the cushion, pushing against him. He thrusts inside her with abandon, over and over into her depths. She continues to moan as he's wracked with the need to come. His heart and blood race as she breathes and coos her release.

It's only moments before he follows her over the edge.

Chapter 18

Bridgette sits in front of her computer. She can't concentrate on the colors and shapes of the safety brochure she's supposed to be laying out. She doesn't give a fuck about Collins Brothers Shipping and their five-step process to safe shipping every day. Though her client was gracious enough to give her an extension in light of her travel situation, all she can think about is New Orleans and Henri. She misses him since she left his house in the Uber with Bunny and Mike. Since she kissed Henri's sleepy face while standing on the curb. He'd held her so close in their last moments together she could still feel his arms around her.

The flight had gone by in a flash. She and Bunny whispering in low voices about what they did in the days they were apart while Mike dozed in the window seat. Bunny giggled at everything Bridgette said, making exaggerated faces at the best parts. Bridgette blushed more often than she ever had.

The memories of recounting her time with him caused an ache in her chest.

She'd snapped a couple pictures of him with her phone and spent more time than she cared to admit scrolling through them. Then there was the video. Her secret, guilty treasure. The last evening they were together, he thought she was sleeping. She had been. But she woke to the soft sound of an acoustic guitar paired with gently falling rain floating through the open window. Henri sang slightly above a whisper the words of Ray LaMontagne's "Hold You in My Arms."

She watched him through the lace panels as he sat on the chaise and played, unaware of his audience. She snuck her phone from the bedside table and recorded him until her guilt forced her to stop. Then she lay there, cocooned in his bed, listening to his beautiful voice.

Her heart had been so full she could hardly feel bad about recording him, capturing those special moments. There are so many recounted moments when her heart and body longs for him to the point of addiction. She played the video once until the emotions filled her chest to bursting, then she studied his smiling face on her phone. For such a boastful character, he has the most humble smile.

Get back to work. she reprimands herself, as her thoughts tipped dangerously to booking a one-way ticket to New Orleans. Printouts of clean lines and shapes in red, blue, and yellow, plastered with words and pictures she couldn't care less about lay spread on her floor. The brochure needs to be eight pages. She has nine worth of content, and they want all the colors and design elements to stay the same. Bridgette's eyes glaze over. The pages blur on the floor around her. She wants the muted, shabby colors of old buildings with crumbling walls and curving balustrades. She wants sticky air that smells of flowers. She wants music on every corner. She wants a smooth Southern voice in her ear. His soft lips on her skin.

"Hey, Bridge?" A voice comes through the door accompanied by a rapid knock. It's Lucy. "Can I come in?"

"Sure." Bridgette sighs at her boring work as she gathers the pages spread on the floor. "I'm never going to get this done."

"How's it going?" Lucy looks around the mess that is Bridgette's work space. Lucy's dressed in skinny leopard print pants and a low-cut black top. Her bright red hair is combed back into a high, slick ponytail.

"Not good. I've got to get my head back in it, but it's so boring," Bridgette whines to the ceiling as she drops the neat stack onto her drafting table that doubles as a desk.

"I hear ya. You got a minute?" Lucy's voice changes from its normal happy tone to a more serious one. "Have you heard anything about the drama that happened over the weekend?" She raises an eyebrow as she sits on the foot of Bridgette's bed.

"No, what happened? No one's said anything." Bridgette sits back in her desk chair.

Lucy lets out a long, heavy sigh, blowing up into her bangs. She settles into a deep slouch and scrunches her lips in a pouty sneer. "We lost The Luna." She blinks a couple times and blots at the corner of her eye.

"What?" Bridgette asks louder than she intended. Her heart beats wildly as she assesses the gravity of the situation. "What do you mean? How? We've been performing there for two years."

"I know. I'm not sure what happened exactly. Cindy got a call from Charles telling us this would be our last show. Something about management having a change of heart."

"What does that even mean? He's the management. We sell out every single show. They make so much money off us. I don't understand. How could they have a change of heart after two successful years? What about our contract?"

"Our next show is the last one we're contracted for. This is the time of year when we renegotiate." Lucy shrugs and shakes her head. "I wish we would've had more notice. I mean, we've already started planning our holiday show. I don't even want to think of the money I've invested in red and green feathers."

"I still don't understand. Did they get religion or something? I mean why would they walk away from all the business we bring them?"

"I don't understand it either. Cindy knows more about it, but not much. She'll be home soon. I wanted to tell you before I left today. You've been holed up here in your room since you got back. We all figured you needed to decompress. I couldn't wait any longer." Lucy stands to leave. "I'm not really sure what we're going to do."

"Yeah. Me either." Bridgette's throat is dry, her thoughts careening and messy. She can't fully grasp a single one before another starts calling for attention. Like a hall closet with items stuffed and stacked haphazardly, if she pulls at one, the whole mess will come tumbling out.

She opens her arms to Lucy, giving her a weak hug. "We'll figure this out," Bridgette says without conviction.

"Yeah. I suppose we will." Lucy sighs before giving a weak smile with her painted black lips. "We will." She nods and heads out the door.

"Love you," Bridgette calls from where she stands.

"Love you too," Lucy calls from down the hall.

Bridgette stands in her room, looking around at her mess. No wonder she can't focus. Her bags sit half unpacked in front of her closet. Her dresser holds all the toiletries and trinkets she acquired on her trip, and then some. Her worktable is covered with printouts, notebooks, pens, and markers. She needs order to work, and a clear mind. Now with the news of the theater and thoughts of Henri ever-present, a clear mind is as far away as Mars.

What are we going to do without the theater?

***

Henri walks with Bones down the broken streets of the Garden District. He's humming the melody of one of Jo's songs on the way to meet him to talk about the demo. It's dusk, the sky is a deep lavender with orange and pink clouds streaming from the low-hanging sun. Annunciation Street is full of folks enjoying the unseasonable break in the heat. Children and dogs play in yards full to bursting with flowers and vegetables. The air is alive, sweet and verdant. Jo sits on the porch of his peach-colored shotgun house with its faded teal corbels and shutters.

"Henri," he calls from his perch.

"Hey, Jo," Henri calls back, approaching the stairs.

"Come on up here, boy," Jo says to Bones, who's wagging his tail furiously at the sound of Jo's voice. Henri drops his leash, and the dog bounds up the stairs two at a time. "How'd it go with your angel?" Jo asks, scratching Bones on the head as Henri joins them on the porch.

"It was heavenly." Henri smiles, taking a seat beside him. Jo offers him a cold, dripping can from a small cooler at his feet.

"That's not what you're here to talk about though, is it?" He sips at his green and white can of Dixie.

"You know me too well," Henri says, settling into his seat. Bones sits beside him, panting happily. "Did you listen to the demo?"

Jo sips silently, looking out over the bustling neighborhood. "I did." Henri watches him with bated breath. The man gives nothing away. Then, a smile cracks on his ageless face. "You were right, man. I didn't believe you, but you were right," he says, shaking his head with laughter in his voice.

"Really?" Henri leans forward, ecstatic.

"Yes, really. I was blown away by the sound quality. Never heard my work like that."

"That's fantastic," Henri says, with a hearty swallow of the chilly beer. "You ready for the next step?"

"What's that?" Jo asks with suspicion in his tone.

"Well, my angel happens to be a graphic designer with an impressive portfolio."

"And?"

"She agreed to work on a branding package for you."

"A what?" Jo laughs his gravelly laugh and shakes his head again.

"A brand package. She can make album cover art, a website, run social media pages, even videos."

"Come on, Henri. What?"

"I didn't expect you to like this part any more than you did getting in to record. But think of the possibilities. You said you liked the sound. Now imagine the full package. Think of your music in homes across the world."

"You've got a hell of an imagination."

"I do. So does Bridgette. I promise. She'll do you justice."

"Then what?" Jo asks, watching his shoes kick at dried leaves on the ground.

"Then, we get you on the radio. Even better, the internet. We get your music out into the world where it belongs."

"Hmm." Jo looks at him with a playful glint in his eyes.

"Jo, this could be something big."

"That's what you always say." He laughs.

"And you always laugh. But I was right about recording you. Why not trust me with this?"

"I think this has more to do with your angel than it does with my music," Jo says.

"It has to do with putting two brilliant artists together to make something amazing."

"Hmm."

Henri falls back into his seat with a sigh. "You are impossible." He points a finger at Jo and before he can say anything, his phone rings. It's Bridgette. He smiles and stands to walk away. "It's my angel," he says with a wink before answering. "*Ma cher,*" he answers, pushing feeling into the endearment. "I was just talking about you."

"Really? To who?"

"Jo. I think he's down for the next step," Henri says, eyeing Jo, who swats at the air and digs in his cooler for a fresh beer. "He's excited about the cover art."

"That's good. I am too. I'm having a hell of a time getting anything done up here."

"I'm sorry," he says, happy to hear her voice. "Any way I can help?"

"Not unless you can make safety brochures and online menu layouts exciting," she answers in a flat voice.

"If anyone can, it's you, *cherie*." He smiles and paces along the sidewalk.

"That's the problem. I can't. I can't make any of this exciting. That city of yours ruined me." She laughs. Henri's heart bangs in his chest. If only he could see the smile that accompanies that laugh. If only she'd say he ruined her for any life but one with him.

"It does that."

"There's something else," she says, her voice low, the laughter gone. Henri braces for what's to come. She's going to tell him it's over. That she's done with him. Their romance had been temporary, a holiday fling.

"What's that?" he asks, holding his breath.

"We lost The Luna," she answers, her voice quavering with tears.

"I'm not sure I'm following." His chest loosens and internally he's sighing with relief.

"The theater, The Luna. We've been performing there for two years. They told us over the weekend they aren't renewing our contract, that we're done. They didn't give any reason. After our next show the contract ends and they're not even interested in renegotiating. I don't get it. Our shows always sell out." She was silent for a moment. "I don't know what we're going to do. We've been there for so long. It's our home. It's where people come to see us. Where are we going to perform?" She wasn't crying, but Henri could hear the pain in her words.

"I'm sorry to hear it, *cherie*. If the rest of your troupe is half as good as you, that theater is missing out."

"Yeah," she says with a sniffle. "You're right. They are missing out. I wish I knew why. I wish I understood what's happening. Like they've pulled the floor out from under us with no warning. It doesn't make sense."

"No. It really doesn't. *Tres triste.*"

"Thanks. I'm sorry for dumping it on you. I called to distract myself. Thanks for listening." Henri waits for her to speak again as he watches Jo throw a stick for Bones.

"You can call anytime," he says after a long pause.

"I appreciate it."

"I mean it. Anytime. Bones misses you terribly."

"Does he?" she asks, the smile coming back to her voice. "Well, I miss him too." Silence again. Henri holds the phone to his ear, wishing she were near so he could hold her close and kiss away her lingering sadness.

"I really do think Jo is on board to move forward. When will you be free to come back?"

"I'm not sure now. With the theater and everything, it might be a while before I'm able to get away. We've got to sort this out." Henri's heart stops for a moment. He'd hoped she would hurry back to him as quickly as possible, but her statement is a stark reminder that she has a life without him, and priorities above him.

He clears his throat. "Of course. I wish there was something I could do. I'd love to show you New Orleans in the fall."

"I've never been," she says, her voice trailing off.

"I think you'll love it."

"I'm sure I will. So that's my goal then, I guess. To be back by fall."

"I can't wait, *cher.*"

"Me either." She pauses, he can hear rustling on her end of the line. "Hey, I've got to get back to work. Thanks for the distraction. I'll call you soon."

"I'll be here."

Chapter 19

It's show night. Bridgette sits on a worn couch in the corner of the dressing room. There's a sadness in the air that no one wants to acknowledge. Her troupe mates move through the motions like ghosts as she remembers their first night performing at The Luna. It was Bunny's last night with A la Mode. It was her last performance before leaving her life with them to start a new one with Mike. Bridgette smiles, remembering the way he surprised them all and whisked Bunny away, and how no one questioned it or thought twice about it. Of course, Bunny left. Why wouldn't she? She found something they'd all been looking for, acceptance. She found someone who sees her for exactly who she is and loves her all the more. She found the one person that could replace them all.

Calvin saunters past, heading toward the bathroom, clearly in his own world. His golden eyes set somewhere in the future or maybe the past. Lucy and Cindy are seated at their mirrors, painting their sullen faces. Jessica and Jonathan are unaccounted for at the moment. But that was common. No sense in being early for the last time.

Scores of memories clamor for her attention as she sits quietly, trying to focus her energy and clear her mind. She recalls the many guest performers who came in over the years. Every person who shared their dressing room admired the closeness of their group. They would comment on how welcome they felt and how genuinely happy everyone seemed to be together. And they were right. The small group had been through a great deal. They'd finally found a place to call home at The Luna and loved sharing it with others. She'd been thinking of inviting Lilian, Charley, and Trixie to perform with them in the future. But that wasn't an option anymore. At least not at The Luna.

Calvin comes out of the bathroom, offering her a sad smile. She nods half-heartedly. He approaches and drops his long frame beside her, leaning his head on her shoulder. "This sucks," he says with a dry laugh.

"It really does. What are we going to do? This has been our life for two years."

"I don't know. I'm not ready for it to end."

"Me either." She lays her head on his. They watch Cindy and Lucy at their mirrors while the clock ticks its countdown to their final performance. Cindy narrows her eyes at them in her reflection.

"You two better buck up. This show's gonna be terrible with everyone drooping around the stage. You know what I say? Fuck these guys. Fuck Charles. Fuck this theater. We'll find another venue."

"I don't want to go back to dark corner stages with crappy sound systems and no dressing rooms," Bridgette says, sitting up.

"None of us do. That's why we have to put our best out there tonight and move on. Let these assholes be a stepping-stone instead of a destination," Cindy says, still looking at them through her reflection. She turns in her chair to face them directly. "Did you really think we were going to be here forever? That this was it?" She stares at them, one brow raised. Then she turns back to the mirror. "Because I didn't." She looks at Lucy in the mirror. "There are better places on this street alone."

Lucy nods. "You're right, Cin." Lucy combs her fingers through her bright red hair and takes in her reflection. "Better theaters with more seats."

"For bigger shows," Cindy says to them all. "With better payouts."

"You're right," Bridgette agrees, watching as Lucy and Cindy go back to their makeup.

Bridgett realizes that she hasn't thought past The Luna. She's never thought beyond performing with her friends and enjoying it for what it is. Her future isn't burlesque. It never has been. Her future is traveling the world and working with artists in every corner of it. She longed to document the struggles and success of life in general. To paint and write and photograph her way through life. For the first time since she joined the ranks of Burlesque A la Mode, she realizes how little she has in common with the people who are closest to her.

"Hey, guys." Jessica pushes through the door with a wide smile. She looks from the couch to the vanity mirrors. "We aren't going anywhere."

"What?" they all say in unison. Cindy stands and crosses the room to Jessica. Bridgette notes the look of relief on her face.

"What happened?" Cindy asks.

"The Luna is under new ownership. They bought the theater and all of its contracts."

"That's awesome. But why?" Bridgette says.

"I don't know. I guess they were looking to sell and that's why they didn't want to renew contracts. Turns out someone wanted it as is," Jessica says with a grin, heading to her spot at the vanity.

"Where's Jonathan?" Calvin asks.

"He's talking with Charles, looking for more details about what's next for us."

Bridgette sighs with relief. The weight she's been carrying for days is gone. Lifted only to be replaced with a newer, heavier weight. The realization her path would eventually lead her away from the family she built for herself is heavy indeed. Too heavy to carry with her on stage. She pushes it deep and focuses on celebrating this small victory with her dearest friends.

***

Henri stands outside The Luna Theater in Chicago. The city is bustling, yet dull. Its clean lines and potted plants tell a tale of ordinances and infrastructure. Small, manicured trees grow through painted woodchips in an inane attempt to convince the citizens they aren't living in a well-manicured zoo. He longs for the sweet heavy breath of home, the wild air full of life and mystery. But Bridgette is here. She has, in their short time together, become as precious to him as that sweet, wild air.

Unbeknownst to her, he flew in early that morning to sign the closing documents on the theater. Having looked into it after learning the troupe was losing their contract, he learned it was on the market and reasonably priced. Though he isn't in the real estate business and has no intention of moving to Chicago, he made an offer. With a hefty wire transfer and a few signatures, he's on his way to being Bridgette's hero. He can't wait to see her face again.

To hold her and hear her laughter. The weeks since she left have been painfully quiet and lonely.

He would have to hang around for a few days to get things in order. Which means more time with her. His new ownership will require regular visits to Chicago. Even more opportunities to see her. Maybe he'll look at apartments while he's here. Maybe she'll want to stay in it while he's away. Surely she didn't want to live in a town house with five other people indefinitely. He daydreams as he watches patrons filing into the theater.

The longer he stands there, the more crowded the sidewalk becomes. People lining up at the box office, others passing through to the will call table. Those who had already made it in to buy drinks are back out to smoke and chat, enjoying the late summer evening. Henri begins to think that his spur-of-the-moment decision is turning out to be a sound investment. He starts thinking of looking for a similar place back home. Maybe reaching out to Lilian and her friends, bringing them in as a regular act. He's never thought of owning a theater, but the more he considers it, the more he likes the idea. Eventually the crowd thins out and heads into the small theater. His theater. He laughs at the thought and follows a few stragglers in. His phone bings in his pocket.

We didn't lose The Luna. I can't believe it.

He smiles to himself and types a quick response.

That's great news.

We're about to go on. I'll text you later.

His smile grows as he passes Charles with a nod. It's a small place with a room full of tables. Each seat is occupied by someone laughing, chatting, or grinning. Henri can see the stage clearly from his place at the bar. The noise of the crowd grows quiet as the house lights go down. The stage lights come up on an empty stage. The room is silent. Then horns blast from impressive speakers, accompanied by piano. Jeff Tuohy's "Bourbon Street" plays as the curtain comes up. Bridgette is lined up with four other people, each one dressed in something slinky and black, wearing sparkling fedoras and twirling canes. They step and kick in perfect unison. As a group they are a beautiful cross section of human beauty. One tall and athletic, one with curves for days, another slight and androgynous. There's even a man, long and lean. Then Bridgette in all her glowing perfection with her shapely legs and smiling face.

They move through the song with the grace and confidence of seasoned professionals. The audience claps and cheers. The curtain drops at the end of the song as they throw their hats off stage right.

A man in a suit that has seen better days wanders onto the stage, looking lost and confused. After several moments of awkward interaction with the audience, he smooths his long hair and straightens his tie before introducing himself as the emcee for the night. Jonathan Wayne is his name and he has an easy character about him the audience clearly adores. He jokes and goads, instructing them how to be the best audience they can be, then introduces the next routine.

It's a completely different experience than Henri's first burlesque show. They're celebrating every moment along with the audience. The air tingles with electricity. He's swept away. Then Bridgette is back on stage, dancing with the tall man, Malcom X-tacy. Their dance is sensual, with undeniable chemistry. Henri feels a pang of jealousy as Malcom lifts Bridgette and dips her. Their eyes are locked, their lips share secret smiles. He holds his breath as Malcom peels the shimmering gold dress away from Bridgette's body, revealing her sparkling pasties. The crowd cheers wildly. She falls into Malcom's waiting arms in a theatrical swoon. The music fades as she's carried off the stage. Jonathan appears and announces intermission. Henri orders a drink quickly to beat the coming rush.

He stands off to the side, watching the bartenders work. The reality of his purchase is sinking in deeper. He's responsible for these people now. All the bartenders, sound guys, ticket booth attendants, cocktail waitresses, and managers. It's now his job to make sure they get paid. It's up to him to keep the theater running. He begins looking at the place itself, the walls, the furniture, the stage. Its curtains are faded. The lights could be brighter. The tables are old and dated. He wonders if putting money into these things would make a difference to the bottom line. His head buzzes as he considers the reality of what he's gotten himself into.

Malcom breezes past on his way to the bar. He smiles and nods at Henri. Then Bridgette follows close behind. She doesn't notice Henri at first. He takes full advantage of the moment, watching her walk and talk. The silken robe she wears is cinched tight at her waist. Her hair is pinned up in a mountain of curls. She stops suddenly and sniffs the air. Her gaze lands on him as a broad smile spans her red lips.

"Henri?" She runs to meet him. Malcom looks back from the bar at the sound of her voice. His gaze follows hers and he smiles, shaking his head.

"I know you aren't about to pull a Bunny on us, baby," he calls after her. She waves him away with a flip of her hand, her attention on Henri.

"What are you doing here? Why didn't you tell me you were coming?" She rushes into his arms, and he presses her to his chest, elated. Her hair, crunchy with hairspray, tickles his nose.

"It was a last-minute thing. I figured you were busy today."

"I have been, but I would've liked to see you." She steps back and gives him the head to toe. "When did you get in?"

"Early this morning." Her smile is almost bashful as her eyes sparkle up at him. Malcom comes up behind her, handing her a drink.

"Who's this?" he asks with a voice like velvet, assessing Henri with his golden eyes.

"I'm Henri Dauphine. Bridgette and I met in New Orleans."

"Dauphine?" Malcom asks, cocking his chin. "Dauphine, as in the Dauphine who bought this place?" Malcom's shifting from one foot to the other, crossing his long arms over his chest and sipping his drink. Bridgette's smile disappears.

Henri clears his throat, surprised how quickly word traveled. He looks from Bridgette's tense expression to Malcom's curious gaze. "Yep. That would be me." He nods, swiping his hair off his forehead. Bridgette now appears shocked.

"What?" she asks breathily. She turns to Malcom. "Explain." Malcom sips more of his drink. "Calvin? Answer me," Bridgette insists, ignoring Henri.

"The girls at the bar were talking about the new owner. Called him Dauphine. Said he was handsome. This one fits the bill." Malcolm shrugs and turns to walk away.

She looks at Henri. Tears are running down her cheeks. He doesn't understand why she's upset. He meant to make her happy. To give her and her troupe a place where they'd never have to worry about being thrown out. Her reaction doesn't make sense.

"Henri? What's he talking about?" Bridgette asks in a rough whisper.

"I thought you would be pleased. You were so upset when you told me about The Luna. I saw a way to help, and I did." His heart is breaking over the tears on her beautiful face. He wants to take her in his arms and soothe her, but her expression is one of a frightened child.

"I can't believe you did that," she says, her lower lip quivering She slouches and takes another step back, pulling her robe closed at the neck. "People don't do things like that." She gestures to the crowded theater. "I didn't expect you to..." she sobs out the words, shaking her head. Her cheeks are flushed, and she's completely flustered. She closes her eyes and lowers her chin, then she takes a long, slow breath. "I'm sorry," she says. "I can't do this." Her voice is trembling. Henri feels like he's been punched in the heart and the gut. She swallows and blinks rapidly. "You can't go around buying theaters," she says softly, shaking her head. "This...this is too much. I can't do this." She uses the back of her hands to dab at her cheeks. Henri opens his mouth to speak, but she holds up her hand. "Please, Henri. I have to get backstage and fix my makeup. I'm up next." She shakes her head again. "You need to go. I'm sorry... I can't... Please, go." She seems to force her lips into a tight smile as she's blinking back tears. She walks backward, her gaze doesn't leave his until she bumps into someone, then she turns to walk away.

"*Cher,*" he calls after her. She stops and turns back to him, her shoulders slumped, her face the picture of defeat. All the words he wants to say are lost on the air between them. He doesn't know what to tell her to make this better. "I'm staying at the Langham. Call me. I'll buy you dinner after the show." She offers a tiny smile and a shrug before heading backstage.

Henri watches with a heavy ache in his heart. His mouth is dry. Tears threaten in the corners of his eyes. Malcom appears out of nowhere. With a flippant shake of his head he says, "Well, I thought it was sweet." Then he walks to the heavy stage door.

Henri pays his tab and leaves the theater.

The pain in his chest is more than he can bear.

***

It's two in the morning, and Bridgette hasn't called. Henri sits in his suite at the Langham looking out at Chicago's skyline, dumbfounded. The starkness of his room is overwhelming. He's cold. This city is cold. He yearns for New Orleans. He wants to be home with Bridgette at his side.

He flips off the light and goes into the bedroom and lies on the bed, leaving the blinds open to the twinkling golden lights of the city. He stares at the ceiling, empty, replaying the night's events in his mind. *How could I have gotten that wrong?* he wonders as the hum of the empty hotel room lulls him until he falls asleep.

He spends three days in Chicago sorting out the business at The Luna. No calls or messages from Bridgette, but he waits, hoping. He finds Charles to be a competent manager, despite his lack of imagination. Of the staff Henri meets, he's pleased to find them devoted and hardworking. On the calendar, he sees that Burlesque A la Mode has rehearsal time booked Mondays and Wednesdays every week.

As much as he longs to see Bridgette, he gets the message of her silence loud and clear. *If she wanted to see you, she would've called by now,* he tells himself as he entertains the idea of hanging around long enough to see them work. To see her.

He can't take any more rejection. His heart aches too much, and he hasn't been able to keep anything down except coffee, and that sits sour in his empty stomach.

With no more business to attend to, he returns to the hotel. There are no messages waiting. No texts or voice mail.

Her silence says all he needs to know.

156

Chapter 20

It's been two weeks since the show. Two weeks since Henri swept into town to save the day and she sent him away. Bridgette sits snuggled in her bed, watching old episodes of *The Office*. She's been holed up in her room, hiding from the rest of the house and life in general. She stares blankly at the characters moving on the glowing screen. Her phone rings on the bedside table. It's Bunny.

"Hey."

"When were you going to tell me what happened?" Bunny doesn't sound happy.

"Hello to you too," Bridgette responds.

"Sorry. Cindy told me what happened with Henri. Why didn't you call?"

"What was there to say? Henri bought The Luna."

"And?"

"And what?" Bridgette says with a sigh.

"What happened? Cindy doesn't know much. Only that you came back from intermission crying and not wanting to talk about it. She said Calvin filled her in a little, and that you've been hiding in your room ever since."

"Well that about sums it up."

"What did Henri say? How did it go? They said he left after you talked with him."

"He did. I feel terrible for the way I reacted, but he shouldn't've done that. It was too much. It would've been one thing for him to fly in on a whim and surprise me for the show. That's what I thought was happening when I first saw him. I was so happy to see him. But when I learned what he had done..." Bridgette can't put how she feels into words. "People don't do that." She chokes on the words as they pass her lips.

Up to that moment, she's been denying it. But the reality is, Henri buying the theater terrifies her. "It scared the hell out of me."

She sobs softly, dropping her forehead into her hand. "Like, what's he going to do next?" She regrets the way she reacted and hates that she sent him away. But in the moment all she could think of was how money controlled her parents. In different ways, but each chased the almighty dollar to their downfall. Her mother had danced on the head of a pin to keep cruel, brutal men in her life because they paid her way. Bridgette swore to herself she'd never allow that to happen to her. She'd be her own protector.

Bunny sighs. "I don't know, Bridge."

"What?" Bridgette sniffs and wipes at her teary eyes. She's cried so much her cheeks burn from the salt in her tears. She sits up against the pile of pillows she's been burrowed into.

"Money isn't the same for people like him." Bunny pauses, giving Bridgette an opportunity to respond. When she doesn't Bunny goes on. "Didn't he say that day at brunch he could buy and sell that place and it would make no difference to his bottom line? He's living in a world we don't understand. One where purchasing a theater to make you happy was the same to him as buying you a new pair of shoes."

"But it wasn't shoes."

"I know it wasn't shoes," Bunny snaps, clearly losing patience.

"Okay. I admit, I should've talked to him the next day, but I was too overwhelmed. I know he wasn't trying to buy me, but it felt that way."

Bunny sighs loudly. "Love is a crazy thing."

"It's not love," Bridgette denies quickly, her heart beating like a caged bird at the thought.

"You sure?"

"I don't have the energy for this right now."

"You rarely have the energy for what you need to hear."

Bridgette scoffs. "Why would you say that?"

"Because I know you. I know you hide from the world when it doesn't behave the way you want it to. You want Henri. But you want him waiting in the wings until you're ready to let him in. You're testing him and making him jump through unnecessary hoops. That's not cool, and it's not going to work. He's not going to wait in the wings indefinitely."

"I know. But what I saw in The Luna that night was my dad promising my college tuition then stopping payment halfway through my junior year because he didn't like my major. I saw years of work lost and tens of thousands of dollars of debt I never would've taken on without those promises. I saw someone trying to own me."

"Okay. I hear that. But, Bridge honey, you know Henri isn't your dad. He's never done anything like the shit your dad or your mom pulled. Henri's kind and gentle. What about the generosity he showed you? All the wonderful things *you* told me about him?"

"I know," Bridgette says softly, her head and heart aching. "It's pretty much all I can think about *now*."

"Once, you told me I should listen to the universe when it's talking. Seems you might want to take some of your own advice. People like Henri don't fall from the sky. If he can't make it over the wall you built around yourself, who will? And honey, if you're not there to be the woman he loves, now that he's had a taste of that, he'll find someone who doesn't make him run the gamut to get to her heart."

Bridgette's throat swells from the arrow accuracy of Bunny's words.

***

The sun casts dappled light through fluttering leaves over Henri's mother's garden. He sits sipping sweet tea, watching his nieces and nephews run through the lawn of thick green grass, heading toward an impressive swing set. He smiles after them, his sunglasses hiding the evidence of his reckless days and nights.

"It's so nice to see you, Henri," his mom says as she takes a seat across from him. She's lovely as ever, with a few more silver streaks in her chestnut hair. The fine lines around her eyes and pink painted lips are the only other signs of her age. "How long has it been?" she asks, sipping her tea and watching the kids in the yard.

"It's been awhile," Henri responds.

"What's wrong, honey?" She reaches across the table to pat his hand. Her heavy diamond ring flashes in the sun while the gold bracelet clinks lightly on the tabletop. Laughter drifts from across the lawn. Henri forces a tight smile. She knits her brow and purses her lips, stroking the back of his hand.

"I messed up. I really messed up." He shakes his head, eyes set in the distance beyond the swing set.

"Oh honey. What happened?" She closes her soft hand over his.

"I met someone. She's perfect. And I..." He bites his cheek and swipes at his hair. "I went too far, too fast. And now she's gone."

"Oh Henri," she says, patting his hand lightly again before lifting her hand away and waving it in dismissal. "You always go too far, too fast. I never did understand you." Her words cut deeper into his already pained heart. He flinches internally before taking another long sip of tea. The sweetness can't possibly counter the bitter taste her comment leaves in his mouth.

"I'm sorry, what?" he asks, shaking his head incredulously.

"Well, you never could wait for anything. As a baby you were always wailing for something. Once you could walk, we could never find you. You'd be running around on your own, getting into everything. You even rode your bike down the stairs in the front hall. I don't think you were six years old yet. I should have known then." She shakes her head with a benevolent smile.

"Should have known what?"

"That you were going to be my troublemaker. That I wouldn't have a moment's peace as long as I had you."

Henri's head throbs dully as he listens to her. *Is that why you sent me away for so long?* He knows she sees her explanation as some healthy, good-natured teasing. But it hurts. It hurts to be dismissed so easily by the one person he'd hoped would understand him. She cocks her head to one side and looks straight at him. Her clear gray eyes piercing his dark lenses.

"Henri?" He pulls off his glasses, squinting in the sunlight. She lets out a long breath. "Oh, honey. You look terrible." Her hand goes to her neck to clutch imaginary pearls. "What did she do to you?"

"It's not what she did. It's what I did." Her eyes go wide, her mouth hangs slack.

"You didn't..." Her silence is full of fear and disgust. She stares at him, words forming and falling before they make their way into reality.

"I didn't what, Mom?" He stares at her with rage that's been boiling in his soul for years, but keeps his voice low. "You think I killed her? Think you have to clean up another one of my messes?" he huffs and stands quickly, kicking the seat back onto the slate tiles.

"No. No, Henri. Sit down," she says with a tremble in her voice. "Of course not."

"Yeah. Thanks, Mom. I knew I could count on you." His voice drips with sarcasm.

"Look, Henri. You come here looking like absolute hell, after what? Two months without even a phone call? Talking about some girl being gone, and, and, and you messed up…" She looks back and forth between him and the chair lying on its back. "Sit down. Put those glasses back on. I don't want to see you like that." He does as he's told and stares at the tiles. "I was thinking you knocked up some poor girl and forced her to have an abortion. Or, or cuckolded a powerful man and got caught. I would never…" She fidgets the ring on her finger and pats the table. "You know we don't talk about *that*," she says quietly out of one side of her mouth.

Henri takes a deep breath before turning his face to the impossibly blue sky. "Yeah, Mom, I know. We don't talk about *that*."

"So, what did happen that's got you all riled up?" she asks as though all the ugliness she'd hurled hadn't passed between them. As though she hadn't accused him of several terrible things in a row.

He turns his face back to her and opens his mouth to explain the situation in full. But she goes on talking, no longer interested in listening. There's nothing she has to clean up or worry about. So why bother.

"You know, Henri," she says with all the grace and kindness a mother should have. "If this girl can't handle you already, she'll never be able to." Then she reaches across the table and pats his hand again, offering him a sweet grin and a shrug. "Now you should go clean yourself up. Your father will be home soon and you don't want him to see you this way."

"No, Mom. I think I'm gonna take off. If he can't handle me like this, I don't think he'll ever be able to."

Henri stands and leaves without looking back.

Chapter 21

"What's that?" Calvin asks. He's sitting on the couch, practically swimming in an oversize tie-dyed sweatshirt. His long legs are folded under him. Bridgette's standing in the doorway looking through the stack of mail she's been ignoring for far too long.

"I don't know," she says, dropping the less interesting, standard envelopes on the coffee table and sitting beside him. She holds the heavy manila one in her hand. The return address is New Orleans. A tight ball forms twisting her aching heart. She struggles briefly with the thick glue and paper, then reveals a substantial stack of legal documents, crisp and white. A slip of notebook paper falls out after the stack in Henri's unmistakable handwriting.

Bridgette,

I've enclosed the contract for the management of The Luna Theater. I believe that you and your friends will be able to make something even better out of an already great venue. The terms are clear and simple. You and Burlesque A la Mode are to continue performing there indefinitely. If you like what Charles is doing, keep him on. If not, feel free to replace him. I'll make sure he gets a good reference and small severance. I'll be a rather absent owner. But know that I am always a phone call away if need arises.

Also, enclosed is a contract for the work that we discussed for Jo. I imagine a great amount of it can be done remotely from your home. But if you do decide that you need to do any photography or other work here on-site, your trip will be paid in full. I do hope that you are still on board with this. I truly believe that you can help introduce the world to his music.

Thank you,
Henri Dauphine

Bridgette holds the note in her hand. Though it's written in his lovely handwriting, it's cold and empty. She lifts it to her nose, hoping it may hold some of his scent. Nothing; only ink and paper. The heavy stack of contracts sits on her lap. She skims the management one first and hands it over to Calvin. He looks it over with a grin that sparkles in his eyes.

"This is amazing." He flips through the many pages. "Do you know what this means?" he asks, looking up.

"Yeah." She smiles some and fights the tears. "He's practically giving us the theater."

"He *is* giving us the theater. Looks like he'll be owner in name alone. He wants all profits to go to Burlesque A la Mode."

"What?" Bridgette grabs the stack back from Calvin. "He can't do that."

"He can, girl. And he did." Calvin points to the line stating exactly that. Bridgette takes a deep breath and hands the contract back to him. Her guilt over the way she treated Henri has been weighing her down for weeks. Her insides ache. She deserves to feel like shit. *How can he be so kind after the way I treated him?*

"Well, happy birthday, I guess," Bridgette says with little enthusiasm.

"I don't see why you aren't even the littlest bit excited about this." Calvin goes back to the front page of the contract. "You realize what this means, right?"

"Yeah." Her mouth is dry as she fights tears.

"I don't think you do. Think of what we can do with free rein at The Luna. We can start teaching classes and bringing in bigger names. We can book all the shows and pick and choose the contracts. *We* have a theater. We can do whatever we want with it. We can fire Charles." Calvin laughs with glee. "I can't wait to tell everyone." Bridgette watches as he reads on. She holds the smooth pages of the much smaller contract in her hands. Her eyes blur as she looks down at the words.

"Oh Jesus," she shouts.

"What?" Calvin looks up.

"Look at this." She holds up the second contract.

"Is he for real?" He snatches away the paper from her. "Dauphine Records huh? He wants to pay you twenty thousand dollars for a branding package? Isn't that what you make in a year?"

"If I'm lucky."

"Damn, girl. What did you do to this guy?"

"I don't know. But I don't deserve this and I'm not taking his money."

"You're a goddamn fool if you don't."

"You sure about that?"

"Um, yeah. Stop being so pigheaded."

"You don't understand."

"I think I do. You wanna be Miss Independent. Miss I-don't-need-a-man. Well, you are. And you don't *need* a man. You've proven it time and again. So why not take the money and embrace these opportunities? Think of what you could do with twenty thousand dollars."

Bridgette looks at Calvin and takes the contract back. She reads it through and remembers all the ideas she had had for Jo's album cover. She remembers the afternoon she spent with Henri listening to Jo's music, and how wonderful that day turned out.

"I can't believe he's doing this after the way I treated him."

"I can't believe you're thinking about *not* doing this and treating him right."

***

Henri's reflection tells a terrible story. He looks in his bloodshot eyes and hates what he sees. The once bristly shadow on his chin is well on its way to a beard. The hollows in his cheeks remind him that he hasn't had a real meal in weeks. His stomach churns in the sour way that only a strict diet of alcohol and drugs can produce.

Bones, ever present, whines at his feet. "Yeah, I know. I should get cleaned up." He chuckles half-heartedly and looks down at the dog. As always, he wags his tail. "But first, food."

He leaves the bathroom and heads downstairs with Bones following close behind. In the kitchen, Henri faces the mild destruction caused by his bender. Empty beer bottles and sticky rings left by sloppily poured drinks cover the countertops along with ashes from joints and an open bottle of Xanax.

A bag of dog food lies cut open and spilling out onto the floor. Next to it an empty pizza box with only a grease stain left. "If you're gonna go, go all out." He surveys the mess and opens the fridge. Bones noses around the pizza box then eats from the open food bag. "Well, this is depressing," Henri says to the empty shelves. Then he gives Bones some water and heads to the living room, where he slumps onto the couch. The coffee table looks a lot like the kitchen. He drops to his side and pulls his legs up, curling in like a child, and falls back to sleep.

Time disappears as it does when he crawls into this black hole of heartache he's never experienced quite this way before. Henri wakes on the couch, not sure of how or why. His phone buzzes, muffled in the cushions of the couch.

Your big envelope came today.

Henri waits to respond, watching as the three little dots move on the screen. His mouth is sticky and somehow dry. It tastes like liquor and sleep.

I'm sorry. Really.

The cloud of self-pity and dejection slowly begins to lift with each tiny bounce of those little dots.

I'd like to come soon to get started on some content for Jo.

His heart swells, making the pounding in his head seem manageable.

That is, as long as the offer for separate accommodations is still on the table.

He sighs and feels dejected all over again. He rereads the messages before responding.

Of course, your accommodations will be taken care of. How soon were you thinking?

He waits, holding his phone in his clammy hand, a glimmer of hope dancing on his screen.

I could be there by next week.

The heaviness he'd been carrying since he left Chicago is lifting. She'll be here in a week. He'll do everything in his power to make things right between them.

When you have your plans set, let me know. I'll make the arrangements.

Chapter 22

Bridgette stands, speechless, in the hallway of her home for the week. A long table sits between two windows, greeting her with sweetly fragrant flower arrangements. Their bright colors mimic the autumn leaves outside. Pinks, yellows, reds, and oranges spring out from deep greens and purples. The blooms are a stunning variety from simple carnations, roses, and daisies to exotic bird-of-paradise and orchids of varied sizes. She breathes deeply and knows Henri's responsible for the flowers, and for choosing such a beautiful house. She sighs, admiring the bouquets, wondering how he can be so thoughtful after everything she's put him through.

She allows herself to daydream about him. His scent, the sound of his voice in her ear, his touch on her skin. She moves through the house quietly, wondering if she still has any chance to make things right with him. Maybe he's sick of her shit and this trip is strictly business and the flowers are his way of saying "look what you could have had."

Bridgette turns her watery gaze to the living room. Stylish and cozy with plush blankets thrown over a deep leather couch and giant pillows in rich earth tones, it looks like everything he's given her, done for her: perfect. Through tall pocket doors is the dining room. Its round table holds an even larger floral arrangement, matching those in the hallway. Beside the flowers is an envelope with her name written in Henri's lovely handwriting. Inside is a short note and a debit card with her name on it.

Bridgette,

Welcome back to New Orleans. I hope you find your rental to be ideal for your creative process. I've enclosed a debit card for your per diem use. Please, feel free to contact me if you need anything during your stay. Thanks for coming. I'm looking forward to seeing your

work.
Sincerely,
Henri

Her heart aches at the cold, business-like communication. They hadn't spoken directly since she sent him away a month ago. Their text messages and written exchanges had been short and painfully professional. She longs to hear him call her *cher,* to see the tiny lines alongside his eyes crinkle when he smiles. *What if I called him right now?* she wonders. *And say what? Please forgive me. I'm an idiot.* She shakes her head as she passes through the dining room into the kitchen. It's small but stylish. The fridge is full of mineral waters, wines, and an assortment of meats, cheeses, and pickles that remind her of their first night in his house.

A loaf of crusty bread sits wrapped in brown paper on the counter. She pops open a green bottle and drinks the refreshing fizz straight from it. Then she's back in the hall heading to the rear of the house. The bathroom is small and clean with a short, but deep clawfoot tub and tiny tiles on the floors and walls. The towels are thick and freshly washed. The toiletries are from Hové. *Of course they are.* She opens a bottle of body wash to smell the fresh, sweet scent.

The bedroom is enormous with a king-size bed in the center of one wall. It's buried under mountains of crisp white linens and pillows in muted shades of blue, green, and gray. Across from that is a seating area with a vanity and cream-colored antique chaise. Behind those are French doors leading out to a small porch. From the porch is a wrought-iron, spiral staircase leading to a courtyard surrounded by potted plants that are still flowering despite the changing leaves overhead. The golden light of sunset casts a magical glow to the outdoor space. Bridgette breathes deeply, filling her lungs with the sweet, wild air of the city, overwhelmed by the beauty of it all.

She hurries into the house, through all the rooms to her pile of luggage and equipment. Grabbing her camera, she heads back to the courtyard and snaps picture after picture of every golden angle, every shimmering flower, the broken flagstones, the creeping ivy. She sits on a small footstool of sorts and watches the trees above, blowing in the gentle wind, and captures a video of yellow leaves fluttering over the spiral staircase, landing on the steps and stones. Gradually, the light turns from gold to rose, then deep blue. The air grows chilly. The warm light from inside the French door beckons.

The house is bright and cozy, but there's a draft around every corner, creeping up her back. She realizes how alone she is. Back home, though she likes her privacy, there's always someone around. A bump in the other room made by a dear friend passing through reminds her she isn't alone. Here, there are no dear friends to blame the bumps on. She nibbles on a piece of bread, and it's heavenly. Perfectly chewy, smelling of tangy yeast and sweet butter.

She scrolls through her camera, standing in the kitchen. The images are great. They capture the feeling of the courtyard perfectly. *A courtyard that would be world's better if Henri were lounging there.*

As lovely as the setting is, it doesn't say a thing about Jo or his music. Placing her camera on the counter, she goes to retrieve her phone from the hallway. The windows are dark, and she flips on every switch she passes. Her phone isn't in the hall, her pulse quickens. *Did I lock the door?* She rushes to check. The knob is locked. After securing the deadbolt and the chain, she heads into the living room. Tribal masks hang on the walls with long open mouths and empty eyes. She hurries through, turning on the table lamps.

Her phone is lying on the table beside the open envelope and note from Henri. She flips on the overhead light. The flowers seem to fill up the room with more than their scent. Their warmth and brightness bring a calm to her nervous thoughts. Henri's note says to call if there's anything she needs. *What I need is him to come and make these big empty rooms less empty.*

She picks up her phone, tempted to send a message, but thinks the better of it. Not now. She's too raw. Then, remembering what she wanted it for, she scrolls through her playlists to find Jo's album.

Walking with it back into the kitchen, she finds a Bluetooth speaker to connect to. Jo's music fills the air. She settles on a stool and looks through her camera again. The pictures are too soft for his sound. She needs grit and soul. She needs something dirty and broken, but beautiful. All her pictures bring Henri and his sweet Southern charm back into sharp focus. *Was it the picture or his lingering presence in the house?*

She imagines him setting out the flowers and filling the fridge, knowing he had done it all himself. As she scrolls through the pictures again, she understands what Bunny has been saying about his world and how different it was from theirs.

Buying the theater had been no more to him than the thoughtful gestures he had made today to welcome her back. Though he had stepped well out of her comfort zone, he was so comfortably in his that her refusal to accept it must have been heartbreaking. Evidence of him trying his damnedest to make it right between them has her cringing at her behavior. "Started Something" begins to play over the speaker, filling the kitchen with more than music.

Memories of that day flood Bridgette's mind. Of how he'd come home to her broken and weary. How she held him while he poured his heart out. Then how they made love in his studio. It seemed they'd spent the rest of their time together making love and sharing their hopes and dreams under blankets, tangled together. His smile, so genuine and sweet. So full of trust and…love.

Of course, he loved her. He made it so plainly clear, so obvious, that she'd been a fool to miss it. Here she sits in this beautiful house with lovely flowers and a stocked fridge, feeling like the biggest fool on earth. She chews numbly at the hunk of bread in her mouth and swallows too soon, washing it down with her mineral water. Before she can talk herself out of it, she sends him a message.

***

Henri sits on his balcony watching the traffic roll by. Bones is curled beside him on the chaise. The air is cool with a breeze that flutters the leaves around him. The sky grows dark as his thoughts wander to Bridgette. She should have landed by now and found her way to the Airbnb he picked for her. It was close enough he could be there quickly if she called, but not as close as he would have it. He wanted her here in his house, in his arms. Over the last month, he had played out the scene at The Luna in his mind on repeat. Her haunted expression, how she pulled her robe shut tight and backed away from him. He hated himself for making her feel that way, but even now, he doesn't understand why. Even if the gesture seemed to be too much, she had to know he did it for her. That he'd do anything for her.

The first two weeks after he'd come home had been hell. He tried to drink away her tears. But he couldn't, not until he received that text. It was simple enough. She'd accepted his offer and would be traveling back to fulfill a contract.

That had been his opening. It'd been all he needed to hold on to hope. The hope that led him to painstakingly touring several Airbnb rentals until he found the perfect one. Then filling it with flowers and food, and hope. Hope that she would come around, that she would allow him one more chance to make it right. To bring her back into his arms.

He feels like a madman waiting for any sign that she's arrived and is pleased with his endeavors. That his efforts aren't in vain. The draw he feels borders on addiction. It may not be healthy, but he doesn't care. All he wants is her.

Bing. His phone sounds. It's Bridgette. *It has to be.*

Hey, just got in. This place is beautiful. Thanks for the flowers.
What flowers?
I know they were you.

Again, he hangs on the bouncing dots, wondering if he did the right thing.

They are undeniably you.
Guilty.
Are you busy?

His heart is in his throat. His fingers fly faster than his phone can register.

Not at all. Sitting on the balcony enjoying the weather.
It's lovely.

He waits without patience for her next words.

What's your day like tomorrow?
I don't have much on my schedule. Do you need me?

His heart is full of expectation. Glee bubbles over at the thought of her needing him. Whatever she asks for, he'll do it.

There are a couple sites I wanted to check out, but I'm worried they won't have the right look. I was hoping that you might have something in mind.
I do, actually.
Would you mind taking me?

Nothing could stop me, he thinks as he types his response.

Of course. When should we meet?

I'm meeting Lilian for coffee in the morning. How about after? I'll be waiting for your call.

Henri stands from the chaise, a renewed man. He heads into the house, Bones on his heels.

The message had been almost all business, but there was a bit of flirting.

It was a start.

Chapter 23

Bridgette pulls her coat tight against the cool breeze. Trash and dried leaves swirl around her feet. Lilian waves from her seat on the other side of a large window of a coffee shop. She's wrapped in what looks like a dozen different-colored scarves. Her oversize glasses pair well with the thick knit stocking cap pulled down over her ears. The bell rings on the door as Bridgette passes through. The deep, sweet smell of fresh roasted coffee and baked goods fills her nose. Lilian jumps up to close the distance, wrapping Bridgette in a tight and genuine hug.

"Oh, baby, it's so good to see you again. I missed your face," Lilian says in her low, gruff voice.

"I missed you too. Wish it hadn't taken me so long to get back." Bridgette gives Lilian a tight squeeze. "I love it here." Bridgette takes another deep breath of the delicious aromas.

"I know you do. We love you here too," Lilian says with a wry smile.

"How's it been? What have you guys been up to?" Bridgette asks, peeling off her jacket and checking the chalkboard menu behind the counter.

"Ha. It's funny, actually," Lilian says, her gaze shifting from Bridgette to the ceiling.

"What's funny?" Bridgette asks, stepping toward the counter to order.

Lilian pulls a weird face. "I ran into your friend Henri a couple weeks ago." Bridgette's face warms at the mention of his name, but she can't help but fear what Lilian is about to say. Did they hook up? Given her behavior and the coolness of their communications, he's probably done with Bridgette and has moved on, just like Bunny said he would.

Now worried out of her mind at what Lilian will tell her, Bridgette orders her coffee and takes her seat across from Lilian.

"What happened?" Bridgette asks, attempting to sound like it's all the same to her.

"It was interesting," Lilian answers.

"And?" Bridgette opens her eyes wide and nods.

"Well, I started tending bar at that place we went the first night you were here. Jo was playing, he's a regular. Henri came to see him. We started talking…" Bridgette's stomach turns at what's about to come out of Lilian's mouth. "Turns out he bought a theater."

"Yeah, I know," Bridgette says quickly, irritated Lilian thinks she's revealing something special.

"Yeah? He said he hadn't talked to you about it." Lilian raises a brow. Bridgette's coffee arrives at the table, too hot to drink, but smells amazing.

"No. He didn't talk to me about it. He showed up in Chicago the day of our last show and signed the papers to buy our theater, The Luna. I didn't handle it well."

Lilian looks at her, confused. Her brows scrunch up, her mouth open to speak, then she shakes her head. "He didn't say anything about that," she tells Bridgette. "Why were you upset?"

"I'm an idiot. At the time I was overwhelmed. I had fucked-up parents who had all kinds of money issues. My, ah, coping skills, ah…have been compromised." Lilian dips her chin. "Then, he sends this contract practically giving the theater to A la Mode and changing everyone's lives for the better. He's asked nothing in return. I don't believe he's real sometimes."

"Hmm." Lilian looks down at her nearly empty cup. "That's not the theater I'm talking about. He bought one here." Lilian returns her gaze to Bridgette's.

"What?" Bridgette sets her cup down with more force than she intended.

"Yeah. It's kinda run-down, but he's got plans for renovations. He asked me if I'd be interested in building a troupe and producing shows on the regular." Bridgette's mouth goes dry. Her brain is muddled. She stares at Lilian and knows she should respond, but words fail her. "I talked to Charley and Trixie and they were both down. So, we're doing it. I didn't know about Chicago."

"But…but…" Bridget struggles to find the right words. "He wants to start a burlesque theater here?"

"Not strictly burlesque. He said mostly music. But he wanted to add burlesque to the lineup. Said he'd recently fallen in love with the art form."

"Huh." Bridgette looks at her coffee, contemplating. "Did he say anything about me?" Now her pride has gone out the window. Lilian looks slightly uncomfortable. She stands to get a refill.

"Not really. Only that you were coming down to do some work for Jo's album." She shrugs and walks to the counter.

Bridgette's stomach starts bubbling. *Why wouldn't he say anything about a new theater to me? Because you told him to go away.*

"He's not as big of a dick as I thought," Lilian says as she takes her seat across the table. "He's actually kind of a sweet guy, once you get to know him. So, what's going on with you guys?"

Bridgette stares at the coffee stain on the rim of her cup. "How much time do you have?" she asks with a dry laugh.

"All morning."

*   *   *

"You've got me for one hour, Henri," Jo says, looking up, one hand shielding his eyes from the sun, the other holding loosely to Bones's leash. Henri looks down from his position on a parapet made of rusted metal and rough-hewn wood. He grins from behind several rows of small bells.

"Come on, Jo, have a little fun," he calls as he flicks at the bells. They chime like a child's toy. Bridgette will be there any minute to take photos of Jo. Henri's heart is bursting with joy. He looks up at the deep blue sky dotted with cartoon clouds. The air is perfectly cool and crisp while the sun warms his skin.

"Looks like you're doing all right without me," Jo calls back then walks away, mumbling under his breath. Bones jumps up to follow him close, wagging his tail and sniffing every makeshift standing drum and worn, rusty bench. Henri smiles after them and surveys his surroundings. The Music Box Village is a secret little spot at the end of Rampart Street. It's a favorite place of his, one he regretted not taking Bridgette to on her first visit.

He smells the river from the other side of the walls made of corrugated tin roof sheets. It's a magical playground filled with an assortment of instruments made of random items. Plastic barrels, kitchen sinks, pots, pans, and bowls make up drums scattered about the area on different wrought-iron and wooden stages. A swing sprinkled with tinkling bells swings in the breeze. Ironwork is on display everywhere, showcasing various string and brass instruments. Wind chimes of all sizes sing in the breeze. Strings of lights hang overhead. Jo and Bones have settled on a bench near the entrance.

Bridgette appears and eclipses the shabby magic of the musical playground. Her smile lights up every face it greets. Henri watches as she approaches Bones and Jo with her camera around her neck. They chat briefly before Jo nods in Henri's direction. She turns her face to him. The wooden bridge beneath him feels like it falls away as their gazes meet. She shines like a million stars at once and he's breathless. His heart beats louder than the drums beneath him could. She gives a shy wave in his direction and cocks her head. Henri hurries down the shaking stairs to greet her properly.

"How's Lilian?" He takes Bones's leash from Jo, knowing if he didn't he would find a way to touch her.

"She's good. Seems you two have been busy becoming friends and opening theaters," Bridgette says.

Was that jealousy he heard? "Ah, yeah. I was going to tell you," he says, pushing his hair out of his eyes.

"Why didn't you?"

"You've been busy." He shifts his gaze to Jo and back to her. "It hadn't come up yet." *It would be hard to tell you when we haven't been talking.*

"I'd like to see it, if you have time this week. Lilian said it's got a lot of potential."

"Of course. Yeah." Henri keeps wrapping and unwrapping the leash around his hand. He looks at Jo, still sitting on the bench, watching them with curiosity. Henri hadn't filled him in on what happened in Chicago. "So, what do you think?" he asks, gesturing to the park around them.

"This is perfect." She looks around with the joy of an artist finding a new medium. Her tone shifts from casual to professional like a switch has been flipped. "I'd like to get a couple shots of Jo walking around if that's all right?"

"Whatever you need, angel." Jo stands and dusts off his shirt and pants. "But I ain't too pretty." Bridgette starts snapping pictures of his back walking away. She follows him out of earshot while Henri holds back, still wrapping the leash around his fingers.

He watches as she approaches Jo and starts directing him on where and how to stand, and notices Jo relaxing into his natural posture. He hadn't been thrilled about a photoshoot. "I make the music, Henri," he'd said when Henri visited him the night before. Reluctantly, Jo had agreed to the Music Box shoot.

Now, though, it seems he's actually enjoying it. He strums at strings and leans on an iron phone booth. He's singing into the mouthpiece, his voice projecting over the park. Bridgette takes a video and stops to watch it with a pleased grin.

Henri settles onto the bench with Bones beside him and watches her work her magic. She turns her camera on him and snaps a few pictures, then smiles and turns back to Jo.

Chapter 24

"Bye, Jo. It was really great to spend time with you," Bridgette calls as he and Henri walk away. She's sitting on a bench scrolling through the pictures on her camera. The Music Box Village was the perfect place for their shoot. She has more than enough images for the album art. She's looking through a particularly great set of Jo trying not to smile, and her own grows as she scrolls through them quickly for a stop-motion animation of his sober face cracking into a glowing grin. His playful nature shines beautifully.

The next set she stole while his guard was down. He was admiring one of the many musical sculptures, apparently thinking she was shooting elsewhere. He's the definition of stoic. She imagines the photos in black and white and can't wait to get back to the house to start editing her favorites.

Henri comes back and sits beside her, giving her shoulder a gentle nudge with his own. Her body responds to his nearness. "How'd you do?" He leans back into polite territory. The pleasant fall air seems ten degrees cooler.

"Great. This was the perfect place to do the shoot. Jo is amazing." She scrolls through more pictures. "Look at this one," she says excitedly, showing Henri a picture of Jo leaning against the inside of the phone booth, mouthpiece against his ear. Bones is sitting, looking up at him with his head tilted, his ears perked. Henri leans in to see better. Bridgette catches his cologne for a moment before he leans away, looking as proud as if he took the picture himself.

"That's about perfect right there." He turns his attention to Bones sitting at her feet. "You're iconic now, Bonesy." He chuckles and pokes at the dog's haunch with his polished shoe.

"You really like it?" she asks, full of pride for having captured so many great images and pleasing Henri.

"I really do. Can't say I'm surprised though." She looks up with a smile, basking in his compliment.

"Thanks."

The wind wraps them up, suspended in time, music floats all around. Tinkling bells, clinking chimes, drumbeats, and horns play a cacophonous melody. Every kiss they've shared, every embrace, floods her mind. She's overwhelmed, confused, and anxious. Never in her life has she longed to be held by another person more than she does in this moment. She's lost in him and in the magical makeshift world he brought her to.

Instead of leaning in to kiss her, he clears his throat. The magic is lost. His rejection rings like a hundred cymbals crashing at once.

"Are you hungry?" he asks, cool and calm. She feels drained by the day's events. Her camera feels heavy in her hands, and sticky from her sweaty palms.

"Not really," she lies, not knowing if she can tell him everything in her heart. "I had something earlier with Lilian." She turns her attention back to the camera to avoid eye contact. "Honestly, I think I might head back to my place so I can get these images uploaded and start editing. I've got so many to work with."

Henri leans back on the bench, dangling the leash loosely beside him. Bones lies at his feet. She steals a glance in his direction. His eyes are on the sky. His mouth is set in a tiny frown. She wants to wipe the frown from his face, to see him smiling and playful again.

"I'm also pretty tired. Didn't sleep great last night." She immediately regrets any mention of sleep. Sleeping brought to mind her bed, which brought to mind him in it and the many dreams she's had about him over the last few weeks.

"Huh." He grunts to the sky. "I haven't known you to turn down a meal." Then he chuckles and stands. Bones stands too. "Can I escort you home?" He slides his hands in the pockets of his smooth slacks.

"Uh. I think I'll be all right," she says quickly. "I can get an Uber pretty quick." She holds up her phone with the app already open.

Henri purses his lips and nods. "Well, then I'll wait with you until it gets here." He moves to sit down. She springs up quickly, collecting her things. She wants to throw herself into his arms, to tell him how sorry she is for the way she treated him, but she doesn't know how, and she's frightened it's too late.

"You don't have to. I'll be fine," she says, holding up her phone again. "My driver is already on his way." Henri looks taken aback. She tucks her phone into her jean pocket and gives him a tight smile. "I'm sorry, maybe tomorrow we can get dinner or something. I'm really beat today."

"Sure. I understand." He shakes his head with his brow knit then gives a nonchalant wave of his hand. "Let me walk you out at least," he says with a small smile.

"Okay," she responds, attempting brightness. "This place really is amazing."

***

"Damn it, Bones," Henri says to his constant companion. "I don't know what to do around her." Bones climbs on the couch, circles twice, and curls up, eyeing Henri with a skeptical twitch of his brow whiskers. "What do you think I did wrong?" Bones shifts with his eyes closed, turning his back on Henri, clearly pouting about the long walk they had after leaving the village. "Well, you're no help."

Henri turns on the television and begins searching for a distraction. The remnants of his takeout dinner are spread on the coffee table before him. *She's so close. Should I text to make sure she arrived back safely?*

It'd seemed like she was warming up to him again. Like she was willing to give him another chance. But he must've misread her. He'd thought for a moment that she wanted to kiss him, to be kissed by him. "Why didn't I do it? Why didn't I kiss her? Then at least I'd know. I think rejection might be better than this," he says to Bones, who shifts in response.

"No." He remembers what her rejection had felt like. Flying hundreds of miles and buying a theater to be greeted with tears and to be told to go away. "No, that was worse." *Too much. Too soon.* His mother's words play in his mind. *She'll never be able to handle you.* "Fuck that," he says louder than intended. Bones looks up from his nap, irritated.

"She's here, right?" Henri asks the dog. "I may be alone talking to the dog. But she *is* here. She did fly all this way to work with me. Granted, I paid for the flight and a handsome sum for her services, but she didn't cringe at the sight of me. That's progress. Right?" He stands and begins to pace. "Damnit, damnit, damnit," he says to the ceiling, the dog, the furniture, whoever or whatever will listen.

He clears the table while a movie plays on the television. "Maybe a nightcap," he says on his way to the kitchen, then remembers the sour pit in his stomach from his weeks of drinking heavily and decides against it. He has no intention of wasting what little time he has with Bridgette being hungover. Instead, he heads back to the living room and settles in with his pipe. A quick smoke will take the edge off.

As smoke spirals to the ceiling, he remembers the first time Bridgette came to his house. He smiles at how stoned she got off one hit. Then he remembers the way she told him to kiss her, as well as all the times after that when she insisted that he shouldn't be such a gentleman. "I should've kissed her," he says to the smoke and the ceiling. "I should've kissed her." His text alert goes off. It's Bridgette.

How's it going?

Henri struggles to answer. He types and deletes dozens of words.

Good, you?

I'm all right. Got back and took a nap. Now I can't sleep.

Over the years, Henri has received plenty of these messages. He knows what it means for most women. Bridgette isn't most women. As badly as he wants to be invited over, he can't imagine it's what she wants.

How can I help?

He allows a ray of hope into his troubled mind. His response is open, but not pushy. He waits, impatiently watching his phone screen. If she only knew how excruciating those three dots were.

Can I see you?

He lets out a whoop of joy so quick and sudden he surprises himself. Bones looks up and wags his tail unenthusiastically. Henri's fingers fly with his response.

I'll be right over.

Chapter 25

The ripe cherry tomato bursts in her mouth. Bridgette hums her appreciation, tearing another hunk of bread from the loaf. The nutty mellow cheese that follows is scrumptious. She's tempted to open one of the bottles of wine on the counter, but she waits. Henri will be here any minute. Her nap had been restless. She dreamt of him, of what she should've said or done. Of how differently her night would've been if she had done or said those things. Of why she's so messed up that she can't embrace happiness. Now that she knows he's on his way, she's hungry. Go figure.

The doorbell buzzes louder than she expected. Bridgette jumps with a start and quickly chews and swallows the last bite, washing it down with a hearty swig of mineral water. She checks her reflection in the hallway mirror. *You could have at least brushed your hair.* She pulls it out of the twisted knot that dangles on her shoulder. Running her fingers through the snarls, she looks down at the breadcrumbs on her sweater. "Oh Jesus. I'm a fucking mess," she mumbles as she brushes them off.

Her heart beats rapidly and her mouth goes dry. Down the hall she can see his silhouette against the glass pane of the front door. He's in a pea coat, surely dressed impeccably. "I'll be right there," she calls to the door and watches his shadow swipe at his hair. Her stomach does a pleasant flip at the sight. Her giant worn sweater and leggings will have to do. She can't possibly wait another moment to see him.

Hurrying down the hall, still dusting her sweater, her socks slip a bit on the freshly polished floor. Henri's shadow shifts from one foot to the other. She pauses before opening the door to catch her breath and calm her heart. With a large sigh she slowly undoes the chain, the deadbolt, then the lock on the knob. A cold gust of wind swirls around him and blusters through the open door. His smile is all she sees.

He waits, his hands in his pockets, the collar of his coat turned up against the cold. He dips his head slightly and says, "Hey."

"Hey." Her body is tingling to be so near to him again.

"Can I come in?" he asks, dipping lower into his coat. "It's colder than I thought out here."

"Oh... Yeah... Of course... Please... Yes." Bridgette stammers, stepping aside, opening the door fully. As he passes, she breathes deeply t,aking in the familiar scent she's come to adore. Looking down at herself again, she notices several threads loose on the cuff of her sleeve and pulls them down over her fingers to tuck them away. "You look great," she says to his back as he walks confidently through the house, removing his pristine coat and hanging it on the hook as though he's done it a dozen time before.

"So do you," he says, turning back to face her. "As always." His smile warms the hallway.

"Yeah, right." She spreads her arms wide, then pushes her wild hair out of her face.

"You do," he insists gently. They stand in awkward silence. The weight of their unspoken thoughts swirling around them. She steps toward him.

"Henri, I..." Another step. He stands, his hands in his pockets, head dipped, eyes watching. "I'm so sorry for how I treated you in Chicago. I was shocked and didn't handle it well. But, before that and every day after, you've been on my mind."

"Same about the being on my mind," he says softly, stepping closer to her, his hands still in his pockets. His chin tilts up and his gaze rests on her. They're face to face, their bodies' warmth radiating. Heat creeps into her cheeks. He takes her chin in one hand. *"Je t'aime, mon cher. Je t'ai aime depuis le jour ou je t'ai vu et je le serai toujours."* His voice is low, barely above a whisper.

Bridgette's remedial understanding of French has her certain of some of the words. Her heart dips and dives in her chest. His lips come down on hers, soft, delicate, searching. Then they're gone, leaving emptiness and cool air in their place. Her lids flutter open. He's looking down at her, passion burning in his dark shining eyes. "You've been on my mind every moment of every day," he says, moving his hand from her chin to cup her cheek.

She leans into it, emotions greater than she's ever known welling in her chest. "I don't know what I'm doing, Henri," she tells him with a quaver in her voice.

"What do you mean, *cher?*" He cocks his head to one side, his eyes narrowing.

"I'm afraid." The words fall from her lips before she can stop them. Her mind buzzes, and her heart races.

"Of what?" He brushes her cheek with his thumb.

"Of you. Of this." She holds his hand against her cheek with her own. He takes her free hand in his.

"What's there to fear?"

"Everything." Her pulse is beating wildly in her ears. "I'm not good at this. At opening up. But when I'm with you I can't help it. I want to tell you everything. I want to know everything. I want to swallow you whole. It's the strangest thing I've ever felt." She's still holding his hand in place on her cheek, trembling inside. "I don't want it to end."

His lips twitch with the smile he's attempting to hide. He leans in and stops, his lips hovering over hers. "It doesn't have to," he says before pressing his lips to hers again. The wall she's built so well over the years crumbles under his gentle kiss.

She pulls him closer, her hands on his cheeks. Joy blooms from the rubble of that wall as his arms wrap around her tightly. As their bodies press together, warmth and calm spreads over her. His arms are where they belong. His kiss deepens, and her stomach rolls with pleasant expectation. For weeks she's daydreamed of this moment. Of his touch, his kiss, his nearness. But she wants more. She's been longing for his skilled hands and mouth to work their magic on every part of her body.

As if he reads her mind, he stands straight and leads her down the hallway. Her skin is alive with desire. It tingles from her lips, her cheek, her hand. All the places he's touched before and she can't wait for him to touch again.

She follows, in a dream, admiring the smooth, strong lines of his shoulders as he passes through the house, knowing exactly where he's headed. In the bedroom he turns around, pulling her by her hand against his chest. Her heart thumps wildly. His erection presses against her belly. She pulses deep inside as his lips come down on hers hard and fast, more aggressive than he's ever been. His hands run down her back, cupping her ass, pulling her closer. His tongue darts over hers. She whimpers with excitement, the sound echoes in the open room.

Henri bites at her bottom lip. "I'm addicted to you, *ma cher*," he says in a low growl. His hands leave her body as he starts pulling at his shirt, still kissing her lips hungrily. "*J'ai besoin de vous.*"

She pulls away to tug her sweater over her head then presses her breasts against his heated skin. His lips capture hers again. His hands roam her bare back, pushing down the waistband of her leggings. She tugs at them too, wiggling them off her hips, working them off her feet. She trips in her attempt to do it all while still kissing him. He catches her smoothly and grins when their gazes meet.

She pulls him back to her lips, greedily, then tugs at his belt. He kicks out of his shoes and pants without missing a beat. His thick cock bounces a greeting as he gathers her back to him. Their bodies meet fully in a silken tangle of limbs. They stand together beside the bed exploring one another in a frenzy as if there's a time clock on them knowing each other completely.

His mouth strays from hers to her cheek, her throat, her ear. He whispers something she cannot hear over her rushing pulse. The ecstasy that follows his kisses runs throughout her body. Her breasts scream for attention.

He guides her to the bed, setting himself down and pulling her in. His tongue plays at her swollen nipples while he cups each breast. He laps at them and sucks them fully into his mouth. She drags her fingers through his hair, dropping her head back until her hair tickles the top of her naked ass.

His hands trail from the side of her breasts back to her ass. He cups it again and crushes her to him. His rigid cock brushes her most tender places. Then he stands and guides her forward, stepping behind her. She lowers her body onto the plush bed and waits. His hands knead her ass cheeks, gently at first. Then he squeezes with one hand while his cock brushes her clit from behind.

She's reeling with bliss as he explores her dripping sex with the tip of his. He traces every folded petal of flesh as she squirms beneath him. Then, without warning, he plunges deep, rolling his hips and grinding into her. She bucks against him as his fingers dig into her ass. His hands run over her hips, around her waist, up her back, and settle on her shoulders. He grips them, bending her up and away from the bed. Her back is arched at a delicious angle, exposing her bouncing breasts to the cool air while he pumps wildly.

One hand slips from her shoulder and down her spine, moving slowly around her waist and down to her clit. She pushes against the soft pads of his fingertips while he thrusts from behind, still clutching her shoulder with the other hand.

They grind together in a perfect rhythm. Their breaths seem to be one. She feels the pleasure swirling and building. It's pulsing deep inside her and radiating out from her core. Every place he's touching sings out. She cries and moans as her climax crashes through her until she's hanging limp in his arms as he gathers her close to his chest and rocks her against him. He squeezes her tightly and grinds himself to his own pulsing release.

Panting and weak, they climb into the soft bed. She lies back against the rumpled pillows. He lays his head on her breast. She runs her fingers through his thick, silky hair and smiles at the ceiling. As her breath returns to normal, she speaks quietly. "I'm not sure what this is or where we're going." She takes a deep breath that shudders in her chest. "But I am sure of one thing. I've fallen in love with you and I don't want to go on another minute pretending I haven't."

He lets out the breath he's been holding and snakes his arms around her, squeezing her tightly. "I've never heard a more beautiful sound, *ma cher,* than those words coming from your lips."

Epilogue

Springtime in New Orleans is more magical than Bridgette could've imagined. The sweetness that never fully leaves the gardens moves rapidly to full bloom and overtakes the city with color and fragrance. Bridgette stands outside of the newly renovated Stardust Theater enjoying a moment of quiet in the freshly planted courtyard. A small magnolia tree offers a handful of pink blossoms. Young azalea and honeysuckle bushes display their lovely blooms at her feet. In a few years the new plants will fill the space with beauty and perfume. Bridgette breathes deeply the sweet scent. Her heart is lighter than she's ever known. Inside the theater are hundreds of people celebrating the culmination of several dreams coming together to achieve beautiful things.

The Starlight Theater's opening night includes a release party for Jo's album, *Sinner and Saint,* and the debut performance for The Moonshine Maidens. Lilian, Charley, and Trixie had worked tirelessly on costumes and choreography for a night of magic and mischief at the same time Jo's album was on the charts and rising.

Bridgette has been enjoying her life behind the scenes along with a newfound peace in her heart. She moves through the garden with slow steps, spinning and hopping from one paving stone to the next, her long white dress twirling around her ankles.

"There you are." Henri's voice comes from behind her. His unmistakable scent precedes him.

She turns to see him in a finely tailored blue suit, his crisp white shirt open at the neck. He moves quickly through the courtyard, closing the distance between them. "Always lost in a daydream." He wraps her in his arms. She smiles up at him, ecstatic to have him alone. The weeks leading up to tonight have been busy for everyone, but mostly Henri. He hadn't had a moment to spare.

"This is lovely."

"I thought you would like the courtyard." He looks down with a satisfied smile.

"I don't know how you did this without me noticing." She looks around and wraps her hands around the back of his neck. They sway to the music coming from the theater.

"You've been coming and going through the front doors. It was easy." He grins. She looks into his eyes, and is filled to bursting with a joy she never knew was possible.

"Have I told you how amazing you are?"

"Not today," he teases, lowering his lips to hers, kissing her softly then pulling away. "We have company." Those tiny lines around his eyes crinkle as he nods at the doorway.

Bunny hurries toward her with Mike following close behind. Bridgette's heart jumps with joy. She hasn't seen her best friend since she left Chicago in the fall. Though they've talked and messaged nearly every day since, Bunny hadn't mentioned visiting for the party. Bridgette squeals and runs to meet her.

"Surprise." Bunny giggles and pulls Bridgette into her arms.

"Oh my god, you guys." Happy tears gather in Bridgette's eyes as she hugs back. "I can't believe you're here."

"I can't believe everything you've done since you've been here," Bunny says, pulling away to look her over. "The South has been good to you. You look great."

"So do you." Bridgette wipes at the corners of her eyes, her heart full. "Why didn't you tell me you were coming?"

"It wouldn't be a surprise then, would it?" Bunny lets her go and pulls Henri into a big hug. Mike pulls Bridgette into a hearty side hug.

"Good to see you, Bridge."

"It's so good to see you." She wraps her arms around the width of his broad chest and squeezes before letting him go.

"I have another surprise," Bunny says, skipping back to her and taking her hands. "Look down," she says with a glittering smile and an excited wiggle. Bridgette looks down at their hands. Bunny's sporting a band of sparkling diamonds on her right ring finger. She's bouncing from one foot to the other doing a happy little dance. Bridgette looks up to her smiling face. "We're getting married," she squeals.

"Oh my god. Congratulations." Bridgette pulls Bunny into another tight hug. "How long have you been keeping this from me?" Bridgette asks, sharing a conspiratorial glance with Mike. They've been talking for weeks about his proposal. She helped him pick out the ring via texts with photos. Now she knew why he had been so secretive about how he was going to propose.

"We would've been here sooner, but Mike proposed as soon as we got to the hotel. You can imagine where that got us." Bunny giggles.

Bridgette shakes her head and rolls her eyes playfully. "You're an animal, Bunny."

"You love it. Now come on. I want champagne." She smiles and crosses to Mike, taking his big hand in her dainty one, pulling him away.

"We'll be right there," Bridgette calls, then turns to Henri. "You did that," she says low and smiling, stepping close to him, taking his hand in hers.

"Guilty," he says, brushing her lips with another kiss.

"Thank you." She'd shared her whole past with him, but still, her words hold more weight than he could know. She's not only thanking him for arranging her friends' visit, she's thanking him for changing her life.

For his generosity and kindness.

For sharing the beauty of his soul.

He rests his forehead against hers.

"Anything for you, *ma cher.*"

TURN THE PAGE FOR A SNEAK PEEK AT
BURLESQUE RIVER

BURLESQUE RIVER

"Damn, I'd like to keep that little hula hoop girl on the dashboard of my truck. You know like those little hula girls?" Mike says, leaning toward Vic. The drinks are going to his head. He's taken to talking over the MC in between dancers.

Vic laughs and motions for another round.

"I'm glad you came and dragged me out tonight. Glad I didn't miss this."

"Drink up, buddy." The bartender hands them both a shot of something. Mike knows he'll regret drinking it.

"What the hell. Bottoms up," he says, the shot glass to his lips. "What the…" he lowers the glass and steps away from the bar. "You gotta be kidding me."

"What's up, man?" Vic stands up straight and follows Mike's gaze.

"I thought you'd like her. She seems like you're—" Mike raises his hand, speechless for the moment.

Twelve years. It'd been twelve years since he last saw her. Twelve years since she placed his ring back in his hand and said *sorry* with tears in her eyes. Twelve years since she left him and never looked back. And those years had been kind to her. Back in the day, she'd been all legs and bones. Now she was curves and hips, shimmering in the stage lights like a dream.

Mike rubs his neck. *It can't be.* He steps closer, shaking the buzz from his head. That face, though. It's her. He would know that face anywhere: those eyes, those lips, that smile. How many nights had he dreamt about that face?

His shock fades as cheers and whistles remind him of what's about to happen. He has to fight every muscle in his body not to charge the stage and throw her over his shoulder kicking and screaming. "Bunny Demure, my ass," he says under his breath. Teeth grinding, his fists clenched.

Vic steps behind him. "What the fuck, man? What's going on?"

Mike glowers. "I gotta go." Then he mumbles, "The last shot was poison," and heads for the door.

The heat hits Mike as he pushes outside. Nothing could've prepared him for that. He blows all the air out of his chest, shoves his hands into his pockets, and with his head down heads toward his apartment.

Where has she been? This is what she's done with herself? This is what she left me for? "God dammit." *I'd come so close to forgetting. Should've stayed home.*

Mike hesitates. Inside that club is possibly the most dangerous woman he's ever met. She's held his heart for nearly two decades. Try as he had to let go, he never could. There hadn't been a single woman in all the years that could make him feel the way she did. These days, she wasn't much more than a box full of trinkets and a couple of old snapshots. Who was he kidding? He still thought of her regularly. Anytime someone introduced him to a woman, saying "she's perfect for you," he'd take her out, have a good time, maybe even take her out a few times. But it never worked. He always compared them to her. And she was just on the other side of this door.

He had wondered so many times what she was doing, where she was. Never had this crossed his mind. *Burlesque? Really? It isn't quite stripping, but I thought she had had more respect for herself.*

All of his questions could be answered if he has the nerve to open the door and ask. She'd always worn her heart on her sleeve. No reason to think she wouldn't share her story with him tonight.

But then, how many years had separated them? For all he knows she's married and her husband is sitting in the club waiting to take her home. The damp heat urges him forward, forcing him to open the door. A couple of patrons push their way through, lighting cigarettes and chuckling together about something they'd seen.

"Here goes nothing."

The chill of the a/c hits him, cooling his sweat-dampened shirt. Johnny Tuesday steps down from the sound booth on his way out for a smoke. Six and a half feet tall and tipsy from the drinks he's been generously supplied by the bar staff, he grins at Mike.

"Kick-ass show tonight. We should book these guys again."

"Maybe, John." Mike's response is short. He's on a mission and not looking for small talk.

He scans the room, looking for Amanda. She's standing at the bar, laughing and flirting with Vic. Mike's heart beats heavy in his chest. He's frozen for the moment, not sure how to approach her.

What do you say to the only woman you ever loved, and who disappeared from your life for over a decade and now she's right in your own backyard? Does she know? Only one way to find out.

ABOUT THE AUTHOR

Kitty Bardot juggles a life full of excitement and love. By day, she's a chef with her own catering company, by night she puts ten years of burlesque experience to use in various venues in the Quad Cities. She writes from her country home not far from the Mississippi River, enjoying every moment with her husband and their three children. Currently, she is working on her next Burlesque River story.

Connect with Kitty:
website: kittybardot.net
instagram: @ktbardot
twitter: @KittyBardot
facebook: facebook.com/Kitty-Bardot-312641412082507

www.BOROUGHSPUBLISHINGGROUP.com

If you enjoyed this book, please write a review. Our authors appreciate the feedback, and it helps future readers find books they love. We welcome your comments and invite you to send them to info@boroughspublishinggroup.com. Follow us on Facebook, Twitter and Instagram, and be sure to sign up for our newsletter for surprises and new releases from your favorite authors.

Are you an aspiring writer? Check out www.boroughspublishinggroup.com/submit and see if we can help you make your dreams come true.

Made in the USA
Middletown, DE
12 May 2021

39492488R00108